Last Chance

ANGELA LAM

Publisher: Gross Productions
Cover Designer: Kingwood Creations

Print ISBN: 9798985793581 (paperback)

For Leanne.

Thank you for over thirty years of friendship and love, and for letting me borrow the Chinese version of your name.

Also by Angela Lam

NOVELS

Legs

Out of Balance

Blood Moon Rising

The Divorce Planner

Friends First

The Women of the Crush Series

NOVELLA

No Amends

SHORT STORIES

The Human Act and Other Stories

MEMOIRS

Red Eggs and Good Luck

The Fool and the Magician

"All of us have the capacity to experience real love."

—Sharon Salzberg

Chapter One

Lian Shu turned up the volume on the stereo and drummed her thumbs against the leather steering wheel, humming along with her favorite Ed Sheeran song. After record winter rainfall, bursts of yellow, purple, and orange wildflowers dotted the fields flanking Highway 1 toward Pacific Grove, California. Lian glanced at the navigation screen. A tingle of pleasure rippled up her arms and down her spine. Only one more hour before she would cross the threshold of the inn that launched her travel writing career almost thirty years ago.

When the song ended and Lewis Capaldi started crooning, she snapped off the stereo. She didn't need his sadness. The pandemic had already destroyed her. First, she lost her job at *Getaway* magazine. The inability to travel made her position an unnecessary expense. Writing blog posts about the mental health costs of sheltering-in-place eased her mind but didn't pay nearly as much as the press junkets and roundups she wrote on assignment.

She sighed.

Next to go was her twenty-year marriage. The pressure of too much time and too little space imploded whatever remained of the calm truce she shared with her then-husband. Waiting until the courts reopened to process the divorce only drowned her in bitter hopelessness. The meager settlement left her with enough to start over, but not enough to buoy her spirits. That's why she needed this one-week getaway—to restore her faith in herself and the possibilities of her future.

The warm sunshine flooded through the windshield. She crooked a smile, glancing at the endless vistas of lush green meadows sprinkled with vibrant California poppies, wild irises, sky lupine, and Indian paintbrushes. Her breath hitched. Maybe she'd see the "Magic Purple Carpet" along the Monterey Bay Coastal Recreation Trail. The magenta ice plant bloomed from early April to the end of May. A shot of adrenaline spiked her blood. What if she could turn this little vacation into an employment opportunity? Maybe pitch an article to the same magazine that had let her go.

Before a barrage of excuses flashed through her mind, she used her hands-free device to call her former boss, Jaz Jimenez. When Jaz answered, Lian launched into her pitch. "Remember the first story I wrote for *Getaway's* romantic escapes issue?"

"The one that won all those awards for excellence in reporting?" Jaz asked.

"Yes, that one." Lian smiled, pumped with pride. "I'm on my way there to stay for a week. I wondered if I could write a story about the inn from a thirty-year perspective, a mingling of past and present divided by the pandemic."

"Sounds promising," Jaz said. "But what's your angle?"

Wasn't the pandemic or the historical legacy enough? Frowning, Lian tapped her thumb on the steering wheel. "How about the eternal romance of the place for the summer destination wedding issue?"

"Hmm…sounds a little too vague and overdone," Jaz said. "But I know how you work. Being on location inspires you. So, send me 2,000 words. If I can use it, I'll pay you double what you made before we let you go. And if the article is a hit, you have a job."

A job. Those magic words crackled against Lian's ear. "That sounds wonderful."

"Excellent." Jaz's voice trilled. "Can you have the article ready before you leave? That way, we can arrange for a photographer to join you on the last day of your stay."

A surge of energy vibrated through Lian. Surely, she could track down the owners for an interview, talk to the guests on record, and dig deep into any past and recent events that would add dimension to the story before the week ended. Smiling, she slapped the steering wheel. "Consider it as good as done."

An hour later, Lian almost drove past the inn. The sign by the sidewalk swung in the wind: Valentino Inn where romance meets elegance. She braked and swerved into the cobblestone driveway overgrown with moss. The white lattice roof on top of the carport needed painting. The parking lot was empty. But she expected that much for a Monday afternoon in the lull between spring break and Memorial Day.

Stepping outside, she breathed in the briny scent of the Pacific Ocean. A cool wind whipped her hair across her face. With a hand, she brushed back her long hair and squinted up at the crumbling staircase leading to the faded pink mansion. How could this place be the same magical spot she remembered?

She left her suitcase in the car and grabbed her purse. After climbing the stairs, she rang the bell and squinted through the frosted glass of the locked front door.

A few seconds later, a portly woman unlocked the door. "Yes, miss?"

"I'm Lian Shu. I'm here to check in." She bit her lower lip and hoisted her purse strap higher on her shoulder.

"Please, come in." The woman stepped back, swinging the door wide open.

Stepping across the threshold, Lian glanced around the lobby. The place was preserved like a museum. The same grandfather clock towered beside the swinging door to the kitchen. An antique hutch full of pamphlets and brochures showcased popular places to visit in nearby Monterey. Next to the hutch, the house rules were posted along with instructions on how to check in and out. Tucked in the space beside the winding staircase, a service station offered tea, coffee, and fruit-infused water. As usual, the French doors to the dining room were opened only during dining hours. Directly opposite, the library beckoned with its built-in bookcases, baby grand piano, and chaise lounges.

"I'll get the owner," the woman said. "I can't check you in. I'm housekeeping."

Lian milled about, taking in the faded wallpaper, the thinning carpet, and the worn and scratched hardwood floors. A sinking stone settled in her stomach. The whole place needed a facelift.

She stepped into the library. The musty scent of dusty, old paper perfumed the still air. On the far wall, beside the award plaques for the best inn of the 1990's, hung a framed copy of the article she wrote. Bending, she read the lead paragraph. She smiled at the color photograph of her kneeling beside the four-poster bed accepting a single pink gerbera daisy from the owner's grandson.

"Ms. Shu?"

The male voice startled her, and she spun. Gazing into the man's big brown eyes, she gasped. The boy in the photograph was all grown up. Her gaze traveled from his floppy black hair to the sinewy muscles of his tanned arms. A flicker of heat lapped up her legs. She skimmed past his wide lips and settled back into those big brown eyes. Blinking, she stepped forward and extended her hand. The shock of his skin against her palm melted the years away. "Flower boy," she said.

Chapter Two

Flower boy? No one had called Roman Valentino that nickname in years. He cocked his head to the side and examined the woman. Could she be a distant relative? Not hardly. Although she had dark hair like him, her pebble-colored eyes were shaped like almonds and her skin was slightly yellow. She was also a foot shorter and as thin as seagrass, not tall and curvy like his mother and grandmother had been. She wore a lace dress with spaghetti straps, showcasing her slender arms and delicate collar bones. Tiny sandals covered her small feet and painted toenails. He frowned. Was he supposed to recognize her like she had recognized him?

The woman released his hand and pointed to the picture in the framed newspaper article. "That's us," she said. "I wrote about this place."

He squinted at his younger self. An uncomfortable heat swept up the back of his neck, and his breath rushed out of his mouth. "Lian," he said. His scalp tingled, remembering the way she ruffled his hair when she hugged him goodbye. *I'll be back someday. I promise.*

She stood before him like a mirage. But he had touched her cool, smooth skin in the handshake. She was real.

"Good to see you again." His chest ached. "What brings you back?" He held his breath, waiting for her answer.

She glanced around the ancient bookshelves. "Nostalgia, I suppose." She shrugged, a smile brightening her face. "And work. I was wondering if I could write a follow-up article for *Getaway* magazine's summer destination wedding issue."

Did he hear her correctly? "I'm sorry, but I think you're too late." Why hadn't she returned sooner? "This is the last week we're open." He swallowed against the resistance. "I'm listing the place for sale."

"For sale?" She gaped, and her purse slid down her shoulder. She shoved the leather strap back up. "Why?"

The hitch in her voice echoed against the ceiling. She blinked and spun away, her fingers caressing the spines of the books. Her hips swayed as she strode across the room. "This place has so much history."

Pain lanced his heart. In addition to the history, the inn housed his favorite memories. He rubbed a hand across his chest. But his feelings didn't matter. Only one thing mattered. "Money," he said.

Nodding, she dropped her hand from the shelf. "I know all about money problems." She tugged her lips into a tight line. "I just got divorced." She waved a hand around the room. "Did you inherit this place from your parents?"

Her gray eyes gleamed with interest.

"No, I inherited from my grandparents." He shoved his hands into his pockets. "My dad and mom didn't care about the inn. Too much work. Too little reward." His gut clenched. "When Pop and Nana got sick, they took out a reverse mortgage to pay their hospital bills. The bank will take back the property if I don't repay the loan."

She crossed her arms over her chest and gestured toward the baby grand piano. "What if you sell the antiques?"

"I don't know." He stammered. "I already discussed all my options with my fiancée." Why did he wince when he mentioned Paula? "She said the inn must go."

"There has to be another solution." Lian paced, tapping her chin with a finger.

He wrinkled his forehead. Why was she so interested in helping him salvage this place? He cleared his throat. "I appreciate your concern, but I trust my fiancée's decision." He smiled, and his shoulders relaxed. Paula knew how to manage things. "She's a real estate agent. She says the market is hot right now." He shifted from foot-to-foot. "She's already had tons of investors call, and the inn isn't officially on sale until next Monday."

"One week," Lian whispered. She blinked rapidly and swiped a hand under her eyes.

Something softened inside of him. Was she crying? Over the inn?

"I'm sorry," Roman said. His back stiffened. Why was he apologizing? It wasn't his fault the inn had to be sold.

She grabbed a tissue from the coffee table and dabbed at her eyes.

Her tears prompted a visceral response in his body. He bowed his head and pinched the bridge of his nose. Ever since Pop died in October followed by Nana's death after the holidays, he'd been cursed with crying jags. Sometimes they snuck up on him while he taught in the classroom, greeted guests in the lobby, or talked with Paula. The children didn't know how to respond. The guests stared in stunned silence. When Paula caught the storm in his eyes, she patted his back. "They're in a better place," she reminded him. "Time to move on." Now, the pressure built behind his eyes, and his throat tightened. Even his nose was clogged. He braced his legs, ready for a tidal wave of sorrow to crash over him and drag him into the depths of self-pity.

But a light touch anchored his shoulder. "I'm sorry, too."

Lifting his face, he stared into Lian's misty eyes. The shock of her sympathy steeled his spine. When the wave hit, he dropped his hand to cover hers. Tears streamed down his cheeks, and she pulled him close, burying her face against his chest. He cupped her back and rested his chin against the top of her head. The moisture of his tears dissolved in the floral scent of her hair.

When the crying stopped, he uncurled from the embrace and stepped back to grab a tissue from the coffee table.

She drifted to the far wall to examine the photo of them again.

He rubbed his eyes and blew his nose, then followed her gaze to the boy he once was and the young woman she had been. What happened during those intervening years? The knots in his chest and stomach squeezed tighter. How many years did he wish for her to return? And now she was finally here. Had his grandparents' ghosts sent her to taunt him about his decision to part with the one thing that had brought them all together?

With a deep sigh, he left the room to grab the key to the suite she had booked. His gaze fell on the stack of unpaid bills on the secretary in the office. Grumbling under his breath, he vowed to deal with them this weekend. When he returned to the library, he glanced at Lian. She was older, he could tell, from the lines on her face. But she was younger, too, from the innocence of her smile. A part of him believed she had come back to rescue him and the inn. The other part of him screamed to grow up and be realistic. They weren't those people in the photograph she kept staring at. They were strangers now.

"Here's the key to the Parker Room."

She stared blankly at the skeleton key. "Thank you."

Her voice was hollow. "I didn't mean to cry just now," he said.

"Don't worry." A weak smile wobbled on her lips. "We all need to cry sometimes." She reached for the key.

Heat sizzled up his arm. He wrapped his fingers around her hand and squeezed, branding the touch into memory. "I hope you enjoy your stay."

"I'll do my best." She slipped her hand out of his grasp. Her gaze traveled over his face and his body. "I can't believe you're all grown up." She gulped. "It's almost as unbelievable as this place no longer existing."

His cell phone rang from his backpack in the office. The shrill tune jangled his nerves. "I have to get that." But he stood a second longer. If he left, would she disappear?

"I'm sure I'll see you around during the week," she said.

The statement released him from worry. He darted across the lobby to the office and rifled through his backpack. Swiping the screen, he said, "Hello."

"Where are you?"

Paula's sharp tone cut through the dreamy fog in his mind. "I'm at the inn."

"We have an appointment at four-thirty."

"I know." He tensed his shoulders. "I'm leaving." He slung the backpack over one shoulder. If he didn't have to sell the inn, they wouldn't need to look at wedding venues. They'd get married here.

Paula huffed. "Hurry."

"I am." He glanced across the lobby. Lian still stood in the library bending to examine another artifact she'd found. Seeing her again made him believe in miracles. "Be there in five minutes." He ended the call and tucked the phone in his pocket. A surge of energy powered through him. Maybe, just maybe, all things were possible.

Chapter Three

After receiving the key from Roman, Lian waited until he left the inn before she returned to her car and carried her suitcase and laptop bag up to her room. If she had asked, he would have helped. But she couldn't spend one more moment with him. The little time they had shared resulted in too many tears.

The key turned easily in the lock, but the knob stuck. She jangled it back and forth until the door squeaked open. A blast of briny air from the open casement windows mingled with a whiff of old wool and layers of wood polish. Squeezing past the wardrobe and the bureau, she set her suitcase on the soft mattress of the four-poster bed and the laptop bag on the bureau. If memory served her correctly, the original owners, Mr. and Mrs. Parker, shared this space as their master bedroom in the late 1800's and early 1900's. Later, when Davide and Marisa Valentino purchased the property in the 1990's, they converted it into the honeymoon suite of the inn. A newlywed couple could expect to be welcomed with a silver Victorian bridal basket full of fresh fruit and a single pink gerbera daisy. But Lian wasn't a honeymooner, so she didn't expect the same treatment.

An achy fatigue pooled in her muscles. She yawned and stretched. Maybe she should take a nap. The drive from Campbell lasted over two hours. She peeled back the lace bedspread. The white wooly fibers itched her palms, and her eyes filled with tears. Breathe. The salty air swelled in her chest, and she swiveled her gaze. The twin mirrors above the corner sink reflected her pale face and disheartened expression. Her breath hitched. She would not have her nostalgic getaway. Her throat closed. She would not have her comeback article.

What was left?

Nothing. Just a husk of an inn. And the little boy who had grown up in its shadow.

She closed her eyes and rubbed her forehead. Had she imagined a spark between them once he placed her? No, silly. She shook the thought from her body. He was engaged. To be married. To another woman. He was only being friendly. Nothing more, and nothing less.

Forgetting the idea of sleep, she plopped into the rocking chair. Leaning back, she remembered how five-year-old Roman came into her room each day with a fresh daisy. The empty crystal vase still sat on the marble tabletop beside her. When had it last been filled? Before his grandparents had died? Or after? She could have asked, but she didn't want to know. The truth might be harsher than the lens of her imagination. Right now, she preferred fuzziness to facts.

She breathed in deeply and rocked gently back and forth in the chair. The floorboards creaked, and her ankles cracked. During her first stay, she had been a new journalist, fresh from college, more familiar with the terrain of babysitting than reporting. Maybe that's why she didn't mind Roman rushing at her with his bowl haircut, dimpled cheeks, and pudgy hands, peppering her with questions. *Can you teach me how to read? Can I draw you a picture?* She laughed at the memory. Luckily, the magazine had paired her with a seasoned photographer who guided her into the story through the pictures he took of the inn, the neighborhood, and the Valentinos. Alone this time, she would need to find a new angle to her story or confess the situation to Jaz.

Think, think, think.

Maybe she could write about saving the inn. Surely, Roman had other options than selling, even if he was short on funds. Maybe he could get the county to register the house as a historical landmark. Or he could crowdfund. Maybe he could ask the bank to refinance the reverse mortgage loan. She grimaced. Changing Roman's mind meant convincing his fiancée. And Lian didn't know anything about the woman.

A flicker sparked in her chest. She stopped rocking and straightened her spine. What if she did the legwork? She could talk to the city, set up a crowdfunding website, and investigate business loans. Lost in thought, she gnawed on her lower lip. She had one week to find a workable solution and convince him to change his mind and keep the inn to restore it to its former glory. Could she do it?

Chapter Four

"Why do you want to go to the farmer's market?" Paula set two mugs of coffee on the breakfast table and cinched the belt on her silk robe.

Without glancing up from his laptop, Roman took a sip of the strong coffee. "I need to buy some fruits and vegetables for the inn." He scrolled through Old Monterey Marketplace's website to confirm the hours of operation. The last time he visited the marketplace his grandparents had been alive and operating the inn.

"Why can't Rosa take care of the shopping?" Paula perched on the chair beside him and nibbled her breakfast bar.

The light through the fog outside their windows shone like a gray mist. The same color as Lian's eyes. Roman shifted in the Pottery Barn chair. An uncomfortable heat simmered beneath his skin when he remembered last night's dream. Clearing his throat, he chased away the image of Lian's tongue parting his lips and the softness of her skin beneath his broad hands.

"Roman?"

Blinking to attention, he swiveled toward Paula's stern frown. "I'm sorry." Was he apologizing for being distracted or thinking of Lian? "I just want to do it."

Paula stood and scowled. "Why?"

Inhaling sharply, he rubbed his freshly shaved chin. Tension knotted in his shoulders. Why did she have to know everything all the time? He glanced at her pinched face. Anything he said would arouse suspicion. Five years ago, her fawning attention endeared him. Now that same quality annoyed him. To buy some time, he took another sip of the rich brew. What could he tell her that would be the truth without giving himself away? A slate of emptiness confronted him. Nothing. Absolutely nothing. She had witnessed his withdrawal from the inn after his grandparents died. Why would he get involved now? Swallowing, he envisioned Lian. He didn't dare spark Paula's jealousy, so he improvised. "It's the inn's last week. I want it to be special."

Paula circled behind him where she could gaze over his shoulder at the computer screen.

He flinched at another one of her irritating habits. Since when had he become a watched animal in the cage of their shared apartment? He pressed his back against the chair, giving her a better angle to view the farmer's market's website. "I thought fresh fruit and flowers would honor Pop and Nana."

"Aww, how sweet." She softened her gaze and patted his shoulder. "Your grandparents would be so proud of you. When are you going?"

"At four. I need to get the shopping done early so Rosa can prep hors d'oeuvres tonight."

She circled back to her chair and sat. The front of her robe parted, and her milky skin below her neck showed. "My last appointment is at three," she said. "I'll meet you here and we'll go together."

"Sure." His voice dipped. "Sounds like a plan." He forced a smile. But his stomach twisted. He didn't look forward to her rushing him through the market, checking off each item from a list, never stopping to linger over the firmness of a tomato or the scent of freshly picked lavender.

He snapped the laptop shut and finished the lukewarm coffee. He had to hurry to pack his lunch before grabbing his backpack by the front door. His first-grade students would be learning how to count to one hundred this week. Thank goodness he had remembered to buy stickers.

After rinsing out his mug, he set it in the dishwasher. Just last week he counted down the days to the inn's closure like a child eager for Christmas. Now he glanced at the calendar on the stainless-steel refrigerator and sucked in a breath. Why couldn't he rewind time to before his grandparents died, before he met Paula, before he told Lian goodbye?

Lian rolled over and glanced at the analog clock on the rickety nightstand. She squinted. Was it really ten after ten? Her stomach grumbled. Ugh. She had missed breakfast.

After tossing off the white handmade quilt, she stuffed her feet into slippers and shuffled to the windows. She tugged open the curtains and glanced outside. The marine layer had already burned off the coast. Golden sunshine glittered on the bay. Gentle waves caressed the rocky shore. Tourists holding hands strolled along the Point Pinos

Coastal Trail. Harbor seals barked and swam through the choppy water.

Yawning, she stretched her arms overhead, releasing the tightness in her lower back from sleeping on a lumpy mattress. She groaned. Why hadn't the mattress been updated?

A tiny black refrigerator had been tucked beside the sink. Inside, two mini bottles of water chilled. But she couldn't find a coffee maker.

Grumbling, she gathered her clothes and shuffled into the bathroom that housed the toilet and claw foot tub. Maybe the coffee downstairs was still warm. Naked, she stepped into the clawfoot tub and turned on the pulsing water. Steam filled her lungs, and she sank into the warm suds. If last night's happy hour served as a warning, then breakfast was better missed. How could anyone call slimy cold cuts, limp carrots, and wilted celery sticks hors d'oeuvres?

Humming, she scrubbed away her cares with a rough wash mitt lathered in exfoliating soap made of peaches and crushed walnut shells. Why bother executing any of the ideas she had brainstormed yesterday? This inn was just another ending. Like her marriage and her career.

No, she had a plan. Cleansed, she dressed before the mirrored bureau. The cheerful colors of her pink shirt and denim shorts brightened her spirits. She dragged a brush through the tangles of her long, straight hair. She wasn't giving up.

Downstairs, she pumped coffee into a paper cup and stirred in two capfuls of creamer. She glanced at the swinging door leading to the kitchen, which still smelled of bacon and cinnamon. She pushed the door open an inch. "Anyone here?"

"Yes, ma'am."

Lian stepped back. The voice was thick and strong just like the coffee she sipped.

A moment later, a stout woman in a floral dress and white apron shuffled into the lobby. "I'm Rosa, the cook," she said, wiping her hands in a dish towel. "Mr. Valentino won't be here until this afternoon. How may I help you?"

Rosa's open and inquisitive face seemed friendly and welcoming. A pang squeezed Lian's chest. "I'm sorry I overslept. Do you know where I can get breakfast?"

After glancing around, Rosa crooked a finger. "Follow me." She padded down the hall into the tiny kitchen with its five-burner stovetop and double oven and dishwasher. From the white cupboards, she removed a plate and grabbed some silverware from a drawer. After setting them on the tiled island, she lifted her eyebrows and whispered, "Don't tell anyone I serve you leftovers, okay?"

Smiling, Lian wiggled onto a stool and set her purse and her cup of coffee on the tiles. "Thank you. I won't say a word to anyone." But if the parking lot was as full as it was when she arrived yesterday, there was no one to tell anyway.

Rosa spooned scrambled eggs from a saucepan, forked over two strips of bacon from a frying pan, and plucked a cinnamon roll from a baking tray. With a flourish, she whisked a white cloth napkin from a drawer. "As Mr. Valentino says, bon appétit."

"Merci." Lian smoothed the napkin over her lap and inhaled the sweet and savory scent of cinnamon and bacon before diving into the meal. "Mmm…this is good." The bacon was tender and crispy just the way Lian liked it, and the scrambled eggs were light and fluffy. Even the cinnamon roll with buttercream frosting tasted fresh and warm. She moaned when she swallowed. What a huge improvement from last night's lackluster appetizers. "How long have you worked here?"

Rosa rinsed dishes and loaded them into the dishwasher. "Five years. We were opened part-time during the pandemic. Not everyone sheltered-in-place."

Lian nodded. "Times were tough."

"They still are." Rosa dumped the pots and pans into the sink and filled it with steaming, sudsy water. "Everyone out of work next week when we close."

"Where will you go?" Lian dabbed her lips with the napkin.

Shrugging, Rosa turned off the water and faced her. "I don't know."

The pinched expression tugged at Lian. One more reason to investigate the options to keep this place open. "Do you know why Mr. Valentino is selling?"

Rosa folded her meaty arms over her sturdy chest. "Paula."

"Paula?" Lian crinkled her forehead.

"Roman's fiancée." Rosa threw open her arms. "That woman thinks she knows it all. But she's just a greedy salesperson. She wants to cash out and move on." Huffing, Rosa shook her head. "Marisa never liked her. She called her a hussy."

Intrigued, Lian leaned closer. Why had Roman's grandmother called his fiancée a hussy? "Is she that much of an opportunist?"

"She thinks she's God's gift to the world." Rosa flung the dish towel over her shoulder and pranced around, shaking her hips. "Oh, Roman, you must sell this place. We need the money for our wedding. Don't you want to buy a home for our family?"

Placing the napkin against her mouth, Lian stifled a giggle. Rosa's impression of Paula bordered on a comedy skit. How had the little boy she remembered grown up to attract someone so callow? Maybe Rosa's spite was unjustified. Paula must have some redeeming qualities. "Why is he marrying her?"

"She's hot." Rosa puckered her lips and placed a hand on her hip. "He's young and thinks that's as good as it gets. But he's wrong." She spun back to the sink and scrubbed the pots and pans. "Marisa was right. He deserves someone better."

Lian finished the food on her plate and the cup of coffee. A comfortable fullness tugged against her waistband. "Thank you again for the breakfast." Rosa's forthcoming nature persuaded Lian to confide in her. "Would you be willing to stay on if I can find a way to keep this place open?"

Swiveling, Rosa gaped. "Are you some miracle worker?"

"No," Lian chuckled. "I'm just a travel writer. Keeping this place open would make for a great story."

Rosa shuffled over and grabbed the plate, napkin, and silverware. "How you make it happen?"

"I have some ideas." Lian tapped the side of her head. "I don't want to say what they are and jinx anything." She stood and smiled. "Wish me luck."

Rosa huffed. "You'll need more than luck to convince Paula."

A hint of tightness trailed along Lian's upper back. She straightened her spine and tugged her lips into a line. "I'm not concerned about Paula. I'm only interested in convincing Roman."

Chuckling, Rosa set the dirty plate and silverware into the sink. "You don't know Roman very well, do you? He only listens to Paula."

"Then I'll deal with Paula when the time comes," Lian said. She grabbed her purse. Her first stop was downtown to speak with a city planner.

"You are brave." Rosa made the sign of the cross. Kissing her fingertips, she raised them up to the ceiling. "May God be with you, mija."

Chapter Five

Dressed in a light button-up sweater, Lian trekked down the stone staircase to Ocean View Boulevard. The sun shone warm against her back, but a chilly breeze blew from the bay. She strolled past charming Victorian homes, turning left on 5th Street, then right on Central Avenue. She had forgotten the city was founded as a summer religious retreat until she counted all the churches. After passing the Pacific Grove Museum of Natural History, she strode toward the city offices. Most of the buildings were well maintained, recently painted and sealed against the coastal winds. The small town was nothing like the urban sprawl where she lived. Walking anywhere at any time in Silicon Valley took just as long as sitting in bumper-to-bumper traffic. Here, the briny air and the friendly people in the quaint neighborhoods welcomed her to fill her lungs and stretch her legs. No caustic smog or hasty vehicles rolling through the intersections threatened to ruin her good mood.

Maybe I should move here.

The thought startled her. She had never considered leaving the Valley, but without her ex-husband, Matt, and his family, there was nothing keeping her there. Her own family had fled the Bay Area years ago, scattering like pollen across the country. Her two younger sisters had relocated to Virginia and North Carolina to start their families. Her parents had retired in Arizona. Her closest relatives, two cousins on her father's side, lived in Sebastopol, California, more than two hours north of her rent-controlled studio apartment in Campbell.

By the time she arrived at the two-story red building and clock tower that housed the city offices, she considered searching for places to rent in this quaint town. As a travel writer, she could call any city home base. Most of her time would be spent on the road anyway.

She shuffled across the marble floors, her footsteps echoing in the cathedral-like ceilings. "Good morning," she said, stepping up to the counter.

The older man pushed his black-framed glasses up the bridge of his nose and smiled, showing a gap between his stained teeth. A whiff of stale smoke and maple donuts mingled in the recycled air. "How may I help you?"

Lian read his name tag. "Tim, I would like to know if a building has been or could be registered as a historically preserved site."

"You a real estate agent?" Tim asked.

"No, I'm a curious citizen." Lian straightened the strap of her purse against her shoulder.

"Usually, I get real estate agents asking for things—permits and such. But not curious citizens." He shoved the glasses up the bridge of his nose and tapped on the keyboard of his computer. "What's the property address?"

She rattled off the street address of Valentino Inn.

"Nothing," Tim said.

Of course, the Valentinos wouldn't think of preserving the status of their bed and breakfast against urban development. They hadn't the foresight. Or they hadn't imagined their grandson's desperation. Lian swallowed a frustrated sigh. "How can I register a property?"

"Well, I need to know more about the place." He handed her a brochure detailing the process of applying for inclusion in the historic preservation program. "We can list sites from pre-history through 1902 or 1903 to 1926 or 1927 to the present, if the property retains 90% of the original structural elements."

Lian opened the brochure and scanned the text. "The house was built in 1899 by the Parkers."

"Most of the Parker properties have been destroyed and rebuilt once they divided their estate in the early 1900s." Tim folded his arms on the counter. "They don't qualify for inclusion."

Frowning, Lian stiffened. "Including Valentino Inn?"

Tim chuckled. "That old place used to be a Queen Anne like the bed and breakfasts near Lovers Point Beach. But after Davide and Marisa bought the two parcels, they tore down the main house and rebuilt it. They couldn't decide upon Spanish hacienda or Tuscan order, so they compromised." He shook his head. "That monstrosity sticks out like a sore thumb. Last month, Paula pulled the permits to tear down both structures to build one of those modern spa hotels like you see on Cannery Row."

Paula. Lian bristled at the mention of the name. Who was this woman and how did she wield so much influence?

Lian flicked a hand against the brochure. "Are there any options other than tear-down-and-rebuild?"

Tim shrugged. "You could remodel and restore, but you probably wouldn't want to do that with supply chain issues and cost overruns." He scratched his ear. "Unless you source everything locally. Davide and Marisa were big on importing everything from Europe, from the Spanish tiles to the Italian furniture."

Nodding, Lian considered the option. But her excitement shriveled to the size of a prune. Roman had probably already discussed this possibility with Paula who had discounted the time and cost involved in a renovation. How could Lian convince him otherwise?

"How do you know so much about the property?" Lian asked.

"I worked as a carpenter building the kitchen cabinets and the built-in bookcases in the library. When you're there every day of the week, you overhear a lot of conversations." He crooked his finger and leaned closer. "They ran out of funds before they finished. That's why the home is decorated with early American art and Victorian silver. They went to estate sales and bid on originals for next to nothing."

Lian widened her eyes. Even then, the Valentino family was in dire financial straits. How did they manage to turn the inn into such a success?

"Thank you for your time." Lian slid the brochure across the counter. "I won't be needing this information after all."

Tim folded the brochure and set it aside. "Why the interest in the place?"

The question pierced her. Why, indeed, was she so invested? After taking a moment to consider her motivations, she bit her lower lip. "Nostalgia, I guess." She pouted. "I was the first to report on the inn's grand opening and now it looks like I will be the last to report on it's inevitable ending."

"Ah, don't be so melodramatic." Tim waved his hand. "Times change. You've got to get on with it." He motioned to his tiny space behind the counter. "Look at me. I used to build homes. Now I issue building permits." Winking, he pointed to her. "You, young lady, need to find a new interest."

Indeed, she did. Without bothering to correct him about her age, she stalked across the marble floors of the big, echoey building and exited into the early afternoon breeze. Slipping a pair of sunglasses over the bridge of her nose, she headed toward downtown Monterey and Cannery Row. She always did her best thinking while exploring. Maybe she could brainstorm another alternative to save the inn while being a tourist.

Roman glanced at the digital clock on the stainless-steel stove in the apartment he shared with Paula. Four o'clock. He hunched his shoulders and shoved his fists into his pockets. He should have told Paula he was leaving an hour earlier. Sighing, he paced the length of the galley kitchen. Why bother? She wouldn't have believed him. After all, she had been looking over his shoulder at the farmer's market website. She would have read the hours of operation. Another argument would have sparked, and he was tired of battling with her.

With another glance at the clock, the tension mounted from his shoulders into his neck. He couldn't wait any longer if he wanted Rosa to prepare anything special for tonight's happy hour at the inn. After grabbing his phone off the kitchen counter, he sent Paula a text.

—*Where are you?*—

A moment later, his phone chimed.

—*Listing a house. Gimme 10 minutes.*—

He groaned and stuffed the phone into his pocket. From experience, ten minutes translated into a half hour for Paula.

An uneasy feeling pulsed from his temple to his jaw. How many times had he been through this routine? Whenever he suggested something, she resisted. Whenever she planned something, he complied. The teeter totter of their relationship weighed heavily on her side. He rubbed the rough stubble against his chin and inhaled sharply. Already the clock read four-ten. He had given her the extra time she requested. He should leave. But halfway across the living room, he stopped.

Think, first. Then act.

The phrase he repeated to his students automatically played in his mind. During his lunch time yard duties today, six-year-old Luis had picked up a rock and thrown it at seven-year-old Franklin. Luckily, no one was hurt. When Roman interrupted the fight, Luis dropped his head to his chest and apologized for aiming the rock at Franklin's head.

"I'm sorry," Luis said.

Franklin glowered.

"You don't want to hold a grudge." Roman nudged Franklin's shoulder. "Let him know the apology has been accepted."

Franklin dug his shoes into the playground dirt before extending his hand. "Apology accepted," he said.

The fight ended fairly, and the boys spent the remaining minutes of the lunch break taking turns at tether ball. From the sidelines, Roman smiled at the outcome.

Now Roman ran his fingers through his thick hair, worrying about what words Paula would hurl at him if he left the apartment without her. His jaw tensed, knowing she would likely demand more than an apology for his thoughtless actions. And, right now, he didn't want to deal with another argument that would escalate into something even he couldn't control. He grumbled. Why couldn't he be a child again, free to act under the illusion of no consequences?

He punched his arms into the leather jacket he grabbed from the closet by the front door. He would compromise and send Paula a text from the market, letting her know where she could find him. With the list of ingredients needed to prepare his grandmother's famous tapas in his breast pocket, he left the apartment with an urgency to his steps.

Chapter Six

Paula's key stuck in the lock of the apartment's front door. Grunting, she jiggled it back and forth. Why wouldn't the landlord rekey the lock? Her fingers trembled. Maybe, just maybe, she wouldn't have to worry about the sticky key anymore. Not if Roman agreed to write an offer on the adorable Craftsman-style home located within walking distance of the elementary school.

She removed the key and inserted it again. The property was perfect with three bedrooms, two bathrooms, and an oversized yard. One bedroom could be a home office and the other could be a nursery for the future baby who might arrive sometime within the next five years. Oh, she couldn't wait to share the good news!

After the third attempt, the bolt finally slid back, and the door opened. "Roman, I'm home!" She clattered in the entryway, setting her oversized bag on the hall table and kicking off her heels. "Roman?" She padded in her nylons through the thick white carpet in the living room to the cool linoleum in the kitchen. "Where are you?"

Her scalp prickled. She was late, but she wasn't *that* late, was she? Backtracking across the apartment, she stomped. He was probably holed up in the bedroom, hiding under the sheet, sulking like a little boy. She flung open the bedroom door. The late afternoon sunlight spilled across the unmade portion of the bed and the heap of discarded clothes on the floor. Shaking her head, she bent and flicked a dirty T-shirt and soiled jeans into the hamper. Standing, she yanked the sheet and comforter over the exposed side of the mattress.

No wonder he taught elementary school instead of college. He was just a big kid.

She poked her head into the bathroom. Sometimes he hid in the tub when he wanted to surprise her. She slid aside the shower curtain. An empty stall greeted her. She flared her nostrils. The scent of his aftershave sharpened her senses. Where was he?

Stalking back to the entryway, she rummaged in her purse for her phone. A green light blinked on the dark screen indicating a missed message. The ringer was off from when she placed it on silence after Roman texted her this afternoon. She switched it on and listened to the message. Her shoulders tensed. He was at Old Monterey Marketplace without her.

Why didn't he wait?

Quivering, she punched the speed-dial.

"Hello?"

He sounded as innocent as a child. She didn't have time for his games. "Roman," she huffed. "Are you still at the market?"

A crowd of voices competed over the static. "I'm sorry," he shouted. "I couldn't wait any longer."

"Where are you now?" She shoved her feet into her heels and flung her purse over her shoulder.

"Getting ready to drive to the inn."

Sighing, she fished the apartment key out of her bag. "Okay, I'll meet you there." Thank goodness the inn was only two blocks away. "I have some good news I can't wait to share."

Lian stepped out of the bakery, licking the cream cheese frosting from her upper lip. Mmm-mmm. After a late lunch of perfectly grilled pastrami sandwich on rye from the corner deli, she had ducked into this warm, inviting cubby hole of sugary goodness to purchase the spongiest red velvet cupcake she had ever eaten. The dessert satisfied her sweet tooth but failed to fill the nagging loneliness inside her.

A slight breeze ruffled her hair, and she tucked a few loose strands behind her ear. Over the past several hours, she had browsed the gift shops on Cannery Row without interruption. When she had been married, Matt never liked to step inside anything touristy. "Everything's overpriced," he would say. "What a waste of money." Her enthusiasm shriveled, and she would let him grab her hand and lead her away to whatever interested him—a bronze statue with a memorial plaque, a crumbling building with historical significance, or a musty museum with creaky floors and cobwebs. Now, without anyone to dissuade her, she had roamed every single overpriced shop. She had even purchased a plush sea otter toy to keep her company at night and a sea otter T-shirt because she fell in love with the whimsical design. When she slipped the pink T-shirt over her head and stared at her chest in the store's mirror, she felt "otterly awesome."

Now, with tired feet, she wandered to a lookout to gaze at the quiet water lapping at the rocky shore. During her first visit to Monterey years ago, sea otters bobbed on the waves. Today the sluicing waters carried nothing but sea kelp. From what she overheard in one of the stores, the southern sea otter population hadn't changed since 1977. The rhythmic movement of the current washed over the rocks. Why couldn't her life remain unchanged?

She set her bags next to her feet, crossed her arms against the black iron railing, and breathed in the clean air. Change was supposed to be good, right? Matt had been a decent husband—honest, faithful, and hardworking. But he had not been her soul mate, if such a thing existed. His high expectations always left her feeling not good enough. Especially when she couldn't carry a pregnancy to term. She tensed. He hadn't exactly blamed her for the miscarriage, but he hadn't sympathized with her either. He gave his full attention to work, spending longer hours in front of the computer. Even the pandemic couldn't bring them together when they were sheltering-in-place in the same house. They circled around each other's space, never touching, never communicating, never revealing the pain and disappointment in their hearts.

She shifted her focus back to the waves. The flow of the water calmed her nerves. The fresh smelling air filled her lungs. The chatter of happy families streamed past her. She smiled. No smog. No bumper-to-bumper traffic. No dead-end marriages. Why couldn't life always be this way—simple and satisfying?

Roman shouldered the grocery bags into the lobby of the inn. He shot a glance up the staircase to Lian's room. The muscles in his chest constricted, making it hard to breathe. Was she there? The parking lot housed one vehicle. Was it hers?

"Roman?" Paula rushed toward him from the library. Smiling, she plucked the bouquet of white and pink daisies from the bags. "Oh, how sweet of you." She dipped her head and sniffed. "What a wonderful surprise."

He widened his eyes. She looked so happy. His chest sagged against the groceries. How could he tell her those flowers were for the rooms at the inn?

"I forgive you for leaving without me," she said.

"Thank goodness." He gestured toward the kitchen. "Let me give these to Rosa, then you can tell me your good news." Without waiting for a response, he maneuvered through the narrow doorway and set the bags on the island.

"What's that?" Rosa pointed and frowned.

"Appetizers for happy hour," he said, unloading the fresh fruits and vegetables. "I thought I'd help you make Nana's tapas."

Rosa plucked a tomato. "You have the recipe?"

"Here." Roman removed the folded paper from his breast pocket and flashed a crooked smile.

"You cook?" Rosa raised her eyebrows.

Roman shrugged. "I can, when I want."

Paula sauntered into the room, hugging the daisies to her chest. "How come you never cook for me?" Her voice cut through the conversation.

An uncomfortable heat radiated from the back of his neck, and he rubbed the skin. "I don't know," he lied. Paula preferred takeout at every opportunity. Why bother buying and preparing food only he would eat?

He grabbed a frying pan from underneath the counter and set it on the stove. "Rosa, could you please dice the tomatoes and cucumbers?"

He swung his gaze toward the daisies. Could he sneak one of the pink ones loose to give to Lian? No, he couldn't with Paula clutching them. Maybe he could distract her. "Paula, do you want to help?"

"What are we making?" She stepped toward the island, cradling the daisies to her chest.

"Rosa's making ensalada de pepino," Roman said. "Spanish cucumber salad. We'll make patatas bravas." He nodded toward a bag of red potatoes. "Can you quarter those for frying?"

Paula puckered her lips for a moment. "I hope you know what you're doing."

He chuckled, turning up the heat to warm the olive oil in the pan. "I'm a little out of practice." He checked the spice rack for salt, smoked paprika, and crushed red peppers. He set the spices on the island and grabbed a garlic bulb from the bag. "Rosa, where are the cutting boards?"

"On the rack by the sink." Rosa jutted her chin toward the window. "Give me the garlic. I'll make the sauce. We only have a half hour."

Roman offered Paula a cutting board.

She shook her head. "I just came here to tell you the good news."

He slapped the cutting board on the counter and grabbed a knife. No daisy for Lian. He quartered the potatoes and tossed them into a bowl. "Tell me."

She narrowed her gaze at Rosa. "I was hoping for a little privacy."

He didn't have time for Paula's nonsense. "Nana always said we talk as a family."

"Nana isn't here anymore." Paula glowered.

Rosa kissed her fingertips and made the sign of the cross before pointing toward the ceiling. "Marisa hears everything now."

Paula scowled. "I don't believe in an afterlife. Once we're dead, we're as good as dust."

Shaking her head, Rosa scraped the garlic into a bowl. "Okay. I'll leave as soon as I get the sauce started."

He narrowed his gaze at Paula. "Rosa doesn't have to leave." His jaw ached. How did Nana and Pop manage the peace? "If you have something to say, say it now or wait till we get home."

"How late are you staying?" Paula asked.

He shrugged. He only planned on helping with the appetizers. But Paula's hostility and lack of respect triggered resentment that rooted him to the floor.

"Roman?" Paula's voice tapped his shoulder.

"I'm listening." He dumped the potatoes into the pan. The olive oil sizzled.

"We need to talk. Alone. As soon as possible."

The yearning in her voice unsettled him. "What's the urgency?" He flipped the potatoes and sprinkled a dash of salt.

Rosa joined him at the stove, heating a skillet. "Let me start the sauce, then I will leave you two alone."

Heaving a sigh, he turned down the heat and covered the potatoes. "Only if Paula agrees to babysit the sauce."

Paula pouted. "I'm not agreeing to anything."

"Pobrecito," Rosa whispered, patting his forearm.

Without glancing at Rosa, he nodded. Nana would agree. She never liked Paula. *She's too bossy for you*, Nana always said. *Find someone easy going.* For the longest time, he disagreed. But maybe she was right.

"Are you both talking about me?" Paula took a step closer.

"No, mija," Rosa said. "We're talking about Nana. God rest her soul." After roasting the garlic, she turned down the heat and grabbed a can of tomato paste and a can of vegetable broth from the bags on the island.

Paula harrumphed. "I don't speak Spanish, but I do speak body language." She pivoted on her heels and pointed the daisies toward the door. "I'll meet you in the library."

"We'll finish faster if you help," he said, waving a hand toward the ingredients on the island.

"I don't want to be where I don't belong," Paula said, before leaving the kitchen.

The door squeaked back and forth on its hinges.

"Don't worry," Rosa said, getting out the measuring spoons from a drawer. "You go take care of her. I'll finish." She nudged his side with her elbow. "I know how to make these dishes. I was just quizzing you."

He couldn't leave Rosa alone. Not when he hadn't prepared her for this amount of work. "How many guests are we cooking for?"

She measured the spices and dumped them into a bowl along with the tomato paste and vegetable broth. After whisking the mixture together, she poured it over the roasted garlic in the skillet. "Three. The woman from Campbell who arrived yesterday and John and Jenn from Phoenix who arrived today."

He frowned. The couple from Arizona sounded familiar. He snapped his fingers. Of course, they stayed here every year to celebrate their anniversary in June. "Aren't they a few months early?"

"I called to let them know we're closing," she said. "I thought they would want to say goodbye."

"How thoughtful of you," he said. "Why didn't I think of that?"

"Because you're too busy." She nodded toward the doorway.

His shoulders tensed at the mention of Paula. He lifted the lid and flipped the potatoes again.

"You should go talk to her." Rosa stirred a dash of red wine vinegar and a tablespoon of cornstarch until the sauce thickened and a fragrant mist rose in the air. "I don't like her, but I like you. I want you to be happy. Just like Nana would." She pointed toward the doorway. "Go before she gets angry."

Stepping away from the stove, he grabbed a dish towel and wiped his hands. Rosa better be right. He didn't need any more trouble tonight.

Chapter Seven

After climbing the stone steps to the pink mansion, Lian froze on the landing. Strong words from a man's low voice and woman's shrill cry battered her ears. She crouched, peering through the frosted glass of the front door. Should she leave? Glancing around at the calla lilies blooming in pots and the ivy trailing up the side of the faded blush stucco, she tried to imagine where she might hide until the danger passed. Was there a hidden entry to the courtyard?

A lull of silence lured her. With trembling fingers, she punched the keycode into the pad. The door unlocked, and she stepped inside. A warm scent of spicy tomatoes enveloped her. She ducked into the lobby, carrying her shopping bags, and shut the door.

From the library, the voices rose again.

"Why do you care all of a sudden?" An angry woman wielded a sword of pink and white daisies. Her pretty face was shielded with heavy make-up, and her navy dress suit fitted her curves like armor. Even her glossy heels looked like weapons.

Lian held her breath. Be quiet. But her heartbeat stuttered in her chest. Gripping her shopping bags tighter, she tiptoed toward the staircase.

"Lian."

A man's voice boomed against her back, and Lian paused with a foot on the lowest step. She glanced over her shoulder. Roman hunched in the doorway of the library, his hands thrust into the pockets of his slacks, his forearms bulging from his blue button-up shirt. A pained expression strained his face. She winced, glimpsing the desperation and longing in his large brown eyes.

Gulping, she lowered her foot to the hardwood floor and faced him. Even though he was taller than the daisy-wielding woman, he looked small and defeated. "Hi, Roman."

A muscle twitched in his jaw. "Are you staying for happy hour?"

She bit her lower lip, glancing from him to the mysterious woman, trying to make a connection.

"Yes, I'm staying." She shrugged her laden arms. "Let me put my stuff away then I'll join you."

"Oh, he's not staying," the woman said, shifting her weight to one hip.

Roman narrowed his gaze at the woman. "Please, go home. I'll meet you in a few minutes. I'd like to mingle with the guests."

The woman shook her head, folding her arms tight against her big breasts. The daisies drooped. "I'm staying until you leave."

Sighing, Roman raked his fingers through his mussed-up hair. He grimaced for a moment before gesturing toward the woman. "Lian, this is my fiancée, Paula." A smile strained his face. Turning toward Paula, he waved to Lian.

"And this is Lian. She's the first person to review the inn. She's here to write about its closing."

Lian flinched at the introduction. She wasn't planning on writing anything anymore. But she hadn't told anyone, not even Jaz, about her decision. Shifting the bags from one hand to another, she swept her gaze up and down the length of Paula's body, from the gleaming hair to the polished shoes. So, this was the woman who ruled Roman's life, the one who made all his decisions, the one who convinced him to sell the inn. Lian shoved back her shoulders and extended her hand. "Nice to finally meet." She flashed a tight smile. "I've heard so much about you."

"All good, I hope," Paula said, squeezing her hand.

Lian twitched. "Yes, impressive." Anyone who held Paula in high regard was a coward because she was nothing more than a glamorous bully.

"I've never heard of you," Paula said, tucking a loose strand of hair behind her ear.

Lian broadened her stance. "I'm just a reporter who writes for travel magazines."

"Amazing how anyone in that industry survived the pandemic." Sneering, Paula swept the bouquet around the room. "I'm surprised this place lasted this long."

Bile burned the back of Lian's throat. No wonder Roman had asked her if she would stay. He didn't want to be alone with this insufferable woman. Lian didn't want to either. She itched to climb the staircase and shut her door against the unbearable static emanating from that woman. But the desperate expression in Roman's eyes stopped her from abandoning him completely. "I'll be right back, if you don't mind." She raised her arms and jiggled her bags. "You two don't eat without me." She winked.

A flicker of light danced across Roman's tired face, igniting a spark in Lian's chest. An unexpected heat flashed through her body, and she scampered up the stairs. After unlocking the door, she slipped inside the freshly made-up room. The housekeeper had made the bed and placed a silver square of chocolate on the pillow.

Lian set her bags next to the empty crystal vase on the marble table by the window. From the sink in the corner of the room, she splashed cold water on her face and rubbed her cheeks with a washcloth.

Downstairs, voices rumbled. She pressed an ear to the door and listened. A volley of harsh words hurtled back-and-forth. Her muscles tightened across her shoulders. Years ago, on her first night at the inn, Roman's parents bickered in the lobby. Lian didn't remember what the fight was about, but she did remember Roman's grandfather interrupting. "I'll take care of the boy," he said. "You go home and finish this nonsense." Roman's parents never returned during her stay. Each day, Roman shadowed her, peppering her with questions. He brought her picture books to read and drew her crayoned pictures. She smiled at the memory of how he wanted to impress her.

Now, she inhaled the scent of roasted potatoes from the downstairs kitchen. Her whole body stiffened. No wonder Paula was so upset. Roman might be all grown up, but he still wanted to impress her. She closed her eyes and rested her forehead against the closed door. If only his grandfather were here to break up the fight, then she could go downstairs and deal with Roman. But his grandfather was dead. She shuddered. How would she confront the arguing couple when she didn't know what to do or say?

She pressed her back against the door and slid until she sat on the carpeted floor. Burying her face in her hands, she waited for the voices to stop shouting. She groaned. Oh, why did he still want to impress her after all these years?

Chapter Eight

As soon as Lian disappeared up the staircase, Paula spun toward Roman and narrowed her gaze. "Why did you invite a journalist to report on the inn's closing?"

"I didn't," he muttered. He spread his arms wide with his hands upturned.

The innocent expression on his face suddenly sickened her. "You're lying," she hissed. Ever since he inherited the place, he wanted to restore it to its former glory. But the outstanding balance on the reverse mortgage loan was too much. He tried to refinance to pay off the debt, but he didn't qualify for a new loan. As a last resort, he agreed to sell.

Now this reporter threatened to derail their plans for a new life together, free of this godforsaken place.

Paula dipped her face into the daisies and breathed in their sweet fragrance. Her eyes misted. "You love this place more than you love me."

"No, I don't." Roman glanced up the staircase, then lowered his hands on her shoulders. "Look at me."

She lifted her chin and sniffed, blinking her eyes.

"I love you more than I love the inn," he said.

Did he?

"I swear I'm telling the truth." He squeezed her shoulders.

The strength in his warm hands comforted her. With a deep breath, she nodded. His voice was steady. Time to share her good news. "I found the perfect home for us today." Smiling, she lifted her voice. "My clients agreed to sell to us directly if we can qualify for a loan within the next 48 hours."

He grabbed the bouquet of daisies and laid it on the lid of the baby grand piano. After sliding his hands down her arms, he clasped her fingers. "You know I don't make enough money," he whispered.

"We would apply *together*." Widening her smile, she wove her fingers through his. "I've already talked to Joe, and he says can pre-qualify us as soon as we're ready." She stepped closer and pressed her mouth against his ear. "Please, come with me to look at the house tomorrow." She kissed his cheek and released his hands.

He stepped back, focusing his gaze on something behind her. "Why didn't you offer to get a loan with me when I wanted to refinance the inn?"

She scrunched her forehead. What was he looking at that gave him so much confidence? She glanced over her shoulder and into his grandparents' eyes in the black and white photograph above the fireplace. Heat blazed through her body. How dare they exert their power from beyond the grave? She inhaled sharply. A hot ball of pressure lodged deep in her solar plexus. "Because we can't live at the inn. We need our own home."

He flinched. "The inn *is* my home."

She waved her hand toward the staircase. "You haven't lived here since we moved into the apartment."

He shuffled his feet and shoved his hands into his pockets. "What if I don't like the house?"

Was he serious? "Of course, you'll love it," she said. "It has everything we talked about." She ticked off the reasons on her fingers. "Three bedrooms, two bathrooms, a two-car garage, and a huge backyard. The best part is it's walking distance to your school." She lowered her voice. "I'm sure you'll agree it's perfect once you see it."

Upstairs, a door clicked open.

Something flickered across Roman's face before he glanced over his shoulder.

She followed his gaze up the staircase to Lian's room. Her jaw tensed. What was the connection between those two?

Roman turned, blocking her view with the back of his head.

A patter of feet shuffled down the staircase.

He swiveled and squeezed Paula's hands. "Okay," he said.

The bright smile on his face thrilled her. She flung her arms around his neck and pulled him close for a kiss.

"Wait." He turned away his head, and her lips skidded across his cheek. Stepping aside, he untangled her arms. "You need to agree to something too."

"What?" She froze. What could he possibly want?

He plucked a pink daisy from the bouquet and handed the rest of the flowers to her. "Let me be the host tonight." He rubbed her shoulder. "Go home. Order dinner. I'll join you in an hour. Okay?" Without waiting for a response, he strode across the lobby and held open the front door.

She stared at the pink daisy in his hand. What would he do with it?

The door swung open from the kitchen, and the scent of garlicky tomato sauce and fried potatoes drifted into the room. Rosa shuffled across the lobby and unlocked the French doors to the dining room.

Lian waved at Paula and Roman on her way toward the dining room.

Roman returned the gesture.

But Paula ignored her.

With only the two of them in the lobby, Roman waited at the opened front door. He twirled the stem of the pink daisy between his fingers and tapped his foot against the hardwood floor.

The ocean breeze exhaled into the lobby, and Paula shivered. She clutched the bouquet to her chest. If she pushed back, he might change his mind about tomorrow. But if she conceded, he might write an offer on the dream home.

With a quick nod, she stepped outside. The door clicked shut behind her. The thud echoed in her body. With heavy feet, she descended the stone steps toward the street. She should be floating toward their apartment, high on winning the argument. But that ball of pressure in her solar plexus moved into her chest.

Chapter Nine

As soon as the door clicked shut, Roman felt the house sigh with relief.

"Is she gone?" Lian poked her head from the dining room.

"Yes, she's left," Roman said. His whole body ached like he had spent the last twenty minutes in a wrestling match.

"Gracias a dios," Rosa said, lifting her pressed palms toward the ceiling.

Smiling, Roman strode over to Lian in the dining room. His palms sweated, and his hand trembled when he offered her the daisy. "For the vase in your room."

Taking a step back, she placed her hands up to stop him. "No, thanks." She shook her head, frowning. "You pilfered this from your fiancée."

"No, I didn't." He pinched the stem tighter. "She stole the bouquet from me." With his free hand, he tapped his chest. "I bought those flowers for the inn. When she saw them, she assumed they were for her."

Lian narrowed her gaze. "And you did nothing to correct that assumption."

Chuckling, Rosa walked by with an armful of silverware and napkins. "No one corrects Paula." She set the silverware and napkins on the nearest table and pointed toward the ceiling. "Not even God."

"That's right." Thank God for Rosa. She knew the truth. Roman clenched his jaw. Too bad Lian thought he was lying. He glowered from Lian's pinched face to the delicate petals. Why risk Paula's wrath if Lian wouldn't accept the gift? He dropped his arm to the side, glancing around for the nearest trash can.

Rosa touched his elbow on her way back to the kitchen. "Don't pout, mijo." She nodded toward the daisy. "If she doesn't want the flower, I'll take it home."

He tightened his grip on the stem. Why did he have to be so sentimental? He softened his gaze at Lian. "I wanted to make this last week at the inn special."

Lian lifted her eyebrows. "Are you sure you didn't do it to impress me?"

Impress her. Heat radiated across his cheeks. He dipped his head and sagged his shoulders. From the kitchen, the spicy scent of his grandmother's tapas triggered a wave of nostalgia. He blinked. Not now. Please, not now. The pressure built behind his eyes, and he turned away to scrub his face with his free hand. This whole idea had been a bad mistake.

A gentle hand warmed against his back.

"Rosa, I'll be okay," he said, glancing over his shoulder. But the woman standing behind him wasn't Rosa. It was Lian.

"If you weren't going to tell your fiancée the truth, then you should have let her believe the illusion," Lian said. "Most women appreciate a romantic gesture."

"But not you," he said, staring into her fog-colored eyes.

A rosy blush colored her cheeks, and she dropped her hand from his back and glanced away. "I'm here on vacation. To relax. Not stir up trouble."

He quivered. No matter what she said, she liked him the way he liked her. The sudden insight boosted his confidence, and he extended his arm to offer the daisy one last time. "For you."

She stared at the flower for a long moment before she curled her fingers around the stem. "Thank you." She swallowed. "I'll go place it in the vase in my room."

Her entire face flushed pinker than the petals. He smiled, and the nerves in his skin tingled. "Don't be too long. The food will get cold."

She nodded, scampering out of the dining room. Her body swayed like a reed in the wind, long, lithe, and willowy.

"Too bad you didn't meet her first," Rosa said, nudging his elbow. "She's nice and pretty, and she wants to save the inn."

"She does?" He arched an eyebrow. A lightness filled his chest.

Nodding, Rosa rolled the silverware into the napkins. "She says she has some ideas."

"Like what?"

"I don't know." Rosa shrugged. "She wouldn't tell me." She crooked a finger. "Come see the food."

In the adjacent room, beneath a crystal chandelier, a feast in Victorian silver gleamed, from the spicy potatoes to the cucumber and tomato salad. On the sideboard, Rosa pointed to sliced lemons, limes, and oranges swimming in a carafe of sparkling red liquid. "Roman juice," she said.

He grinned. "What a surprise."

Whenever Roman wanted to drink wine with the guests, Nana made a concoction of cranberry juice and lemon lime soda in a clear pitcher and called it Roman juice. She loved Roman and wanted him to be a part of the inn's experience. When guests wanted to sample the non-alcoholic drink, she added freshly sliced lemons, limes, and oranges and served it in a glass pitcher next to the carafes of wine. The drink became more popular than any beverage on the menu. But when she fell ill, she stopped making the special drink. Roman hadn't tasted the fizzy fruit-filled concoction in two years.

He grabbed a crystal wine goblet and poured a taste. The sweetness of the fresh fruit mingled with the bubbly tang of cranberry juice and lemon lime soda. "Mmm-mmm." He smacked his lips. "When did you find time to make this?"

Rosa placed a finger over her lips. "A chef never tells her secret," she whispered.

The floorboards creaked with the arrival of the first guests.

An elderly couple shuffled into the dining room.

"John and Jenn," Roman said, with open arms.

The tall, rugged man with white hair and leathery skin tugged Roman into his arms. He smelled like the outdoors. "Good to see you, sonny." He patted his back.

Next, Roman hugged the tiny woman with dyed black hair and cat-eyed glasses. "So good to see you again."

She folded him close, smelling of hairspray and talcum powder. She pressed her lips against his cheek in a motherly kiss. Stepping back, she laughed. "I'm afraid I've got lipstick all over you, dear."

"No worries." He smiled and rubbed his cheek, hoping he'd remember to wash his face before he left. No need to arouse Paula's suspicions. "How have you both been?"

"Good." John gestured to Rosa. "This fine, young woman here invited us to say goodbye before you close the inn." He wrapped an arm around Rosa's shoulders and tugged her to his side. "Shame you couldn't keep it open after your grandparents passed."

Frowning, Jenn touched Roman's arm. "I thought you loved this place."

"I do," Roman said, patting her hand. "I just can't afford the expenses." He pursed his lips. How much should he confide in them and how much he should keep private? "The pandemic hurt everyone. We were open part-time for nine months. When we fully reopened, we could only house a fraction of our occupancy." Judging from their sad faces, he decided not to burden them with the mention of the hospital bills or the reverse mortgage.

"Shame," John said, shaking his head. "Real shame."

The floorboards creaked again, and Roman swiveled. Lian looked stunning with her long black hair freshly brushed and her face scrubbed clean of makeup. A burst of happiness exploded in his chest. "You're back." He glided through the introductions, then gestured to the display of food. "Enjoy the refreshments."

Taking Rosa aside, Roman thanked her. "I appreciate you accommodating my last-minute changes to the menu."

Rosa glanced at the guests sitting at the tables overlooking the bay and smoothed her hands over her apron. "Nana and Pop would be proud of you." She twisted her lips and blinked her eyes, fanning a hand in front of her face. "Aye, mijo, I'm proud of you."

Seeing Rosa cry with gratitude softened something inside of Roman. "Where will you go after we close?" he asked.

She shrugged, dabbing the corners of her eyes with the edge of the apron. "No se. But I'm not worried." She pressed her palms together and raised her gaze toward the ceiling. "God will provide."

Roman raked a hand through his hair. Where would Irma in housekeeping and Lorenzo in gardening work after the inn closed? He dropped his hand. If he didn't have a teaching position, he would be jobless, too.

"These appetizers are good, Rosa." John raised his plate and smiled. "Hot and spicy, just the way Marisa made them."

"Thank you." Rosa nodded toward Roman. "He helped."

"I didn't know you cooked," John said.

"You cook?" Jenn lifted her eyebrows. "When did you learn?"

"Nana taught me. Years ago." Roman cut away his glance. He had been too busy with Paula to come over each night to help Rosa cook. He flashed a tight smile. "I'm glad you're enjoying them."

"They're delicious," Lian said between bites.

She sat at the end of the table next to John who nestled shoulder-to-shoulder with Jenn. If Roman took the seat across from Lian, he would block the view of the ocean. Standing awkwardly at the head of the table, he tapped Lian's shoulder. "Where are you having dinner tonight?"

Frowning, she dabbed her lips with a cloth napkin. "I don't know. I can't think of food when I'm already eating."

John leaned over his second helping of cucumber and tomato salad. "Jenn and I are heading over to the Beach House at Lovers Point at seven. You may join us if you'd like."

Nodding, Jenn smiled. "We'd love the company. We always make new friends when we visit here."

"How long have you been coming?" Lian asked.

A proud smile curled John's lips, and he draped an arm around Jenn's shoulders. "Since our honeymoon thirty years ago," he said.

"Wow, congratulations," Lian said.

Roman latched onto the awe in her voice and her strained smile. Some part of her believed in lasting love even though hers ended.

"Thanks for the invite, but I'm afraid I'll have to decline." Lian bowed her head and nudged the potatoes on her plate with her fork, moving them around the thick sauce but no longer eating.

When John and Jenn left a few minutes later, Roman took the vacated seat next to Lian. The cushion was still warm. He clasped his hands in his lap. "I—was—wondering if—" He stuttered and shifted awkwardly in the seat, glancing out the window at the waves then back at her gray eyes. "You might want to have dinner with me tomorrow. To catch up." He rubbed his thumbs together. "We haven't seen each other in what feels like a hundred years."

She suppressed a giggle by taking a sip from her glass. Her steady gaze lingered on his restless fingers. "We're seeing each other now."

"You know what I mean." He leaned back and ran a hand through his hair, hoping he wasn't being too obtuse because he didn't know how to be clear. "I was a kid, and you were just starting out. And now I teach kids, and you're starting over."

"You teach kids?"

The surprise in her voice encouraged him. Smiling, he nodded. "First grade."

"I always thought I wanted kids." She bit her lower lip. "But I can't have them. Something's wrong with my body." She grimaced and balled up the napkin in her hands. "Sorry. That was too much information."

"No, that's fine." He scooted closer. "I want to know these things."

"You do?" She arched an eyebrow.

"Yes, I do." He swallowed. How could he tell her he wanted to know everything about her? Maybe if he had the time. Alone. He could discover her, and she could discover him. Again. He smiled. "So, what do you say to dinner tomorrow night?"

"With your fiancée?" A dark shadow passed over her face.

He gulped, and a wave of heat moved up from his chest into his neck and across his face. "Of course. Let me call her." He cleared his throat and stood, fumbling for his phone.

"No, please don't." She reached up and touched the edge of his shirtsleeve. "I don't want to cause any trouble."

A zing of energy bolted up his arm, then down his chest, before settling deep in his stomach. The shock mirrored the panic in her eyes. He stepped aside, letting her hand fall, and the absence of her touch chilled him. "No trouble." He shook his head, turning aside, letting the lie burn on his tongue. Dialing the number, he paced across the length of the room. "Paula," he exhaled. "I'm getting ready to leave, but I wanted to know if you'd have dinner with me and a guest tomorrow night. At the Beach House on Lovers Point." A moment of silence ached, and he glanced nervously at Lian who stared at the ocean view, her back tall and straight against the antique dining room chair.

"Seriously? Tomorrow night? What if we write an offer on the house?"

"We have to eat," he reminded her.

She sighed. "Who's the guest?"

He bowed his head and lowered his voice. "Lian."

"Is she interviewing us?"

"No, she's…" An old friend, an acquaintance, a first crush? "Just lonely."

"I'd rather not," Paula said.

"Okay, I'll tell her no." He ended the call and tucked the phone into his pocket. Hunching his shoulders, he strode back to the table. He would never know what Lian had been up to all these years, and she would never know how often he had thought of her.

"What did she say?" Lian glanced up, as he sat down.

"Tomorrow isn't good. We're seeing a house we might write an offer on." He clasped his hands between his knees.

Lian nodded. "That's why you need to sell the inn. Whatever's left after the loan's paid off goes toward your new home."

"Right," he said.

"Makes sense." She pursed her lips and shrugged. "Life is full of sacrifices."

"Have you made many?" he asked.

She blinked slowly. "I'm sure I have."

He waited for her to elaborate.

But she only stared out the window at the ocean.

What was she thinking?

Should he ask?

Sighing, she blinked rapidly and crumpled the napkin in her lap. "I thought life would get better once the pandemic ended."

"It has," he said. "I'm back in school with my students. I don't have to worry about testing every day for the virus or wearing a mask full-time or disinfecting everything three times just to make sure it's clean." He leaned back against the chair and uncurled his hands. "Remember when we worried about running out of toilet paper?" He laughed.

She chuckled. "I remember wiping down boxes of cereal with rubbing alcohol and paper towels because the stores were out of disinfectant wipes."

"See?" He nudged her elbow. "Life *is* better now."

Her lips softened into a smile. "You're right," she said. "We can see each other in person instead of behind a computer screen."

Nodding, Roman thought of Nana and Pop. The pressure welled up in his eyes and nose again.

"What's wrong?" She tilted her head and frowned.

He sniffed. "I'm so glad Pop and Nana got sick after the worst of the pandemic was over." His voice caught in his throat. "I can't imagine them dying in the hospital without being able to hold their hands." He rubbed his eyes with his knuckles. "Sorry for dumping on you like that." Why did he keep falling apart? "I just feel comfortable with you." He blinked rapidly. "That's why I invited you to dinner." He glimpsed the question in her eyes. "I wanted to go with just you," he responded. "Not Paula, not anyone else. Just you." He paused. "Will you go out with me one time before you leave?"

Hesitation hitched in her choppy breath. She was like a wild bird. Any slight movement might startle her, and she would fly away.

Finally, after what felt like forever, she clasped her hands to her chest. "How about dinner the day after tomorrow?" she asked.

Every muscle in his body released. Surely, he could get away from Paula for one night. A crooked smile played at the corners of his lips. "The day after tomorrow it is."

Chapter Ten

In the dark gloom, Lian lay in bed, clutching the plush otter. Every time she closed her eyes, the evening replayed in her mind. Paula and Roman fighting in the library. Lian's rude comment about how Roman was trying to impress her. His surprising response. She opened her eyes, and the pink daisy winked at her from across the room.

Her whole body drenched with heat and sweat. She climbed out of bed and cranked the casement windows. Cool air blew into the room. The ocean waves hushed. She flopped onto the lumpy mattress and fanned her face with her hand.

When she closed her eyes, she envisioned Roman. Mingling with the guests. Asking her to dinner. With and without his fiancée. She cringed. Oh, why had she accepted? She rubbed her face with her hands and blinked her eyes. As an experienced adult, she should know better. Fresh out of a long-term relationship, she needed time and space to be alone and rediscover herself. No self-esteem was no excuse for flirting with a taken man, especially an engaged man with a controlling fiancée. She heaved a sigh, rolling onto her side and grabbing the stuffed otter. She needed to focus on why she was here—to relax and write a stellar story to revive her career.

Only she couldn't relax. And that story she had planned on writing didn't exist anymore. She grumbled, flopping onto her other side. How could she convince

Roman to listen to her ideas on how to save the inn when he was intent on buying a house? As a schoolteacher, he couldn't afford to do keep the inn and purchase a home. A house for his future family won. How could she blame him? She probably would have made a similar choice if she had been in his position back when she was married and hoping to start a family.

She squinted at the digital clock. Five A.M. She groaned, tugged the sheet over her head, and closed her eyes. An unbearable heat seared through her stiff and aching muscles. She flung off the sheet and opened her eyes. Why did she tell Roman about her failed marriage and her inability to have children?

Gray light leaked around the curtains. At least, she hadn't told him she was jealous of Paula. But he probably could guess that much from her contradictory actions. Why tell him she didn't want to cause problems only to accept his invitation to dinner without his fiancée?

When her thoughts offered her body no relief, she turned on the hurricane lamp and climbed out of bed. She tugged the new otter T-shirt over her head and wiggled into a pair of jeans. She scrubbed the morning breath from her tongue and brushed her hair until it gleamed. After grabbing her key and tucking her phone into a pocket, she switched off the lamp, shoved her feet into shoes, and exited the room.

In the lobby, she choked down a mouthful of the day-old cold coffee before dumping the paper cup in the trash. She wound through the parlor to the conference room and exited through the French doors. The courtyard lit up with white fairy lights strewn beneath a canopy of greenery surrounding the square. Tucked in a stone cubby hole above a fountain and koi pond, a statue of the Virgin Mary stood with outstretched arms. Her bare feet crushed a serpent's head. "Mary, Mother of God, pray for us" read the inscription above the statue's head.

The protected space was warmer than Lian expected. With her palm, she wiped down dew-like moisture before sinking into a wicker chair. The water from the fountain tinkled into the pond. She breathed in the intoxicating scent of blooming orchids. Soon she would call Jaz in New York City to cancel the article. That would give Jaz plenty of time to reassign the photographer to another story and accept a pitch from another writer to fill the space in the magazine. Lian sighed. Too bad she didn't have any ideas for a replacement article.

"Good morning."

She jerked her head at the sound of a man's voice. Like a wavery mirage or a sleep-induced dream, Roman padded across the courtyard carrying a thermos and two paper cups. She gulped. Why did he look so good? He was dressed in a gray T-shirt and sweatpants. His hair was mussed, and dark stubble shadowed his cheeks and chin. He took a seat at the wicker table and poured steaming coffee into paper cups. The muscles in his forearms flexed, and Lian bit her lower lip to staunch the desire flooding into her mouth.

"What are you doing here?" Lian cradled the warm cup in her hands, already regretting the question. He didn't need a reason. He owned the inn. He belonged here.

Roman gestured to the windows. "I was leaving for my morning run when I saw your light go on." Smiling, he lifted the thermos. "I thought you might like some fresh coffee."

The hot, bitter brew was perfect. "Yes, thanks." She dipped her head and took another sip. His inquisitive gaze swept over her. She shivered. How did she look? Like a sleepless zombie masquerading as an early riser or a lost middle-aged woman?

Roman thumbed behind him. "I live two doors down."

"Mmm-hmm." Lian nodded, lost in his big brown eyes. She set the cup down and breathed in the new earth smell of his skin. Her hands were almost childish next to his. How strong and powerful was he? Could he pin her against a wall with one hand while the other hand explored her body? Her breath hitched. Focus. But her curious gaze caressed the length of his long, lean legs. What did he look like underneath those sweats? An uncomfortable pressure built deep in her gut. He was no longer a little boy. He was a grown-up man.

And he was getting married.

A hint of anxiety inched up Lian's spine. "Where's Paula?" She glanced behind him at the French doors.

"She's at her spin class downtown." Roman took a sip and leaned back in the chair, crossing one leg over the other. "She doesn't like running."

"Neither do I." Lian chuckled, happy to find some common ground with his future wife.

"What do you like to do?" Roman folded his hands in his lap and leaned forward.

Did he really want to know? Lian fiddled with the cup on the table. "Explore new locations around the world," she said. "But during the pandemic, I took up cross-stitching and baking. My apartment is full of tiny pictures of fruit and flowers." She laughed. After removing her phone from her pocket, she showed him pictures. "I got good after a while. Here's a scene of Paris."

When he cupped her phone, he brushed his fingers against her hand.

A zing of electricity zagged up her arm, and she held her breath. The prickles ignited and sparked throughout her body. Moisture flooded to the surface of her skin, and she parted her lips.

As he gazed at her handiwork, his thick, long lashes shaded his eyes.

"Nice," he said, removing his hand. "Did you bake bread like everyone else?"

Shaking her head, she snapped her mouth shut and wiped her damp palm against her jeans before scrolling through more photos. She tapped a picture of a platter of red velvet cookies with cream cheese frosting. "I only experimented with cake cookies."

"Cake cookies?" He quirked an eyebrow, peering at the photo. "How are those different than cupcakes?"

"They're actually cookies but frosted like a cake." She felt like a child showing a parent her creations. "Matt didn't like them. He said they were too sweet." The memory of her ex-husband's judgment soured her, and she tucked the phone back into her pocket. "What about you? What do you do for fun?" She picked up the cup of coffee and waited.

"My whole life is fun," he said. "I get to spend my days with six-year-olds discovering the magic of learning." Smiling, he nodded to her shirt. "We just went to the aquarium last week. The kids loved watching the otters and penguins during feeding time. And they enjoyed the petting pools of sting rays and urchins."

She bit her lower lip, staunching the pain. If the last pregnancy had been successful, her child would be six years old. Old enough to be in Roman's class. Old enough to be at the aquarium. She blinked and shook her head, redirecting her thoughts. She could still have children in her life. Maybe visit her sisters more often and be a more involved aunt. Or volunteer at a preschool. But those possibilities didn't fill the emptiness inside of her. The unbearable loss forced her to ask. "Will you and Paula have children?"

A shadow flitted across his face, and he fixed his gaze on the fountain. "I don't know."

How could he marry a woman who didn't want children? She shifted in the wicker chair. "Doesn't Paula like children?"

He frowned, directing his gaze at her. "It's complicated."

"What do you mean?" She scrunched her face, trying to understand.

"I'm not sure if I want to have children with her."

His gaze wandered over her face and down her body then back up to her eyes again. A quiver ran through her. What did he see? She swallowed, trying to refocus on the conversation. "Why not?"

A muscle tensed in his jaw. "I don't know if I want to marry her anymore."

She gasped. "What changed your mind?"

He poured more coffee into both of their cups. "I don't think we're on the same page anymore." He took a sip and held her gaze. "We haven't been for a long time. But I just ignored it. I think I was hoping the doubt would go away." Shaking his head, he grimaced. "Kind of like I was hoping the bills would go away, and I wouldn't have to sell this place." Exhaling, he leaned forward. "Sorry for the heavy conversation. You probably didn't want to hear all of that."

"No, I'm glad you told me." The confession eased the burden of guilt she felt over her desire. "You need to talk to someone."

Glancing at his watch, he widened his eyes. "I should get going." Standing, he gathered the thermos and his cup. "Do you want the rest of the coffee?"

Shaking her head, she stood. "I'll walk out with you." She wasn't ready to say goodbye. Every moment with him felt precious.

"No, that's okay." He gestured to the table. "You stay here and enjoy the quiet." He flashed a crooked smile, then left with hunched shoulders and a hurried stride.

A prickly sensation traveled from her legs and lodged in the pit of her stomach. Was he going to break up with Paula?

"What do you mean there's no story?" Jaz said.

Lian paced back and forth across the courtyard, one hand gripping the phone while the other hand pressed against her temple. The sharp rise in her former boss's voice ricocheted like a steel ball in a pinball machine, triggering an avalanche of failure that threatened to bury the good vibes of her vacation. She gulped and closed her eyes for a moment to regather her thoughts. "The inn is closing." She opened her eyes and focused on a trellis of honeysuckle weaving up a pink stone arch above the French doors leading to the inn. The powerful scent drew her back to the magic of this place, and she inhaled deeply to find her footing. "I can't report on a destination for weddings when that destination will cease to exist this coming Monday."

"Find another story," Jaz said. "You're in Pacific Grove, right? That's next to Monterey and Carmel-by-the-Sea, two of the most romantic places in California. There's bound to be another bed-and-breakfast you can interview for the story." The click-clack of fingers flying across a keyboard filled the space. "Here's a potential lead. The Gables. I want you to check it out. See if it's related to that book *Anne of Green Gables*. If it is, we can use it for the Top Ten Literary Places to Visit This Summer. Got it?"

Dropping into a wicker chair, Lian gazed up at the slate gray sky above the courtyard and considered the offer. She had enough money from the divorce settlement to get her comfortably through winter if she wanted to pass on this story. But the prospect of a potential staff position with all expense-paid trips, health benefits, and a 401(k) plan tempted her. She had already gambled on love and lost. Why not take a chance on this proposition?

A niggling sensation prickled her scalp. What about Roman? She nibbled on her lower lip. Why was she concerned about him? Even if he broke up with Paula, it didn't mean he wasn't selling the inn.

"Okay. I'll look into it," Lian said, injecting a smile into her response.

"Great," Jaz said. "Get back to me as soon as possible with whatever you find. I'm counting on you to deliver a one-of-a-kind story."

Chapter Eleven

Roman released the seatbelt, stepped outside of Paula's SUV, and stood outside the walkway to the modest Craftsman-style home amid a row of grander residences three blocks from the elementary school. The late afternoon sunlight created a glow around the roof, casting shadows in the garden full of blooming lupines and poppies. A breeze kicked up, cooling the nervous energy buzzing about him. He shoved his hands into his pockets. Paula was right. The house was cute.

"Great curb appeal," Paula said, locking the doors of her vehicle.

He winced. Why did she have to talk to him like he was a client?

She tugged his hand. "Come see inside."

The front porch had been rebuilt with a manufactured wood and plastic material that didn't need to be resealed against the salty air. Nice. Inside, the owners kept the interior arches between the living and dining rooms to give the home an authentic turn-of-the-century feel while updating the space for modern living. He nodded, touching the plaster walls with his fingers. The kitchen had been updated with stainless-steel appliances and laminate flooring. Standing at the kitchen sink, he pulled back the curtain and gasped. An expansive lawn extended to the fence with enough room for a dog run, a swing set, and a barbeque and picnic area.

"What do you think?" she asked.

A few trees sheltered the backyard like the stucco walls of the courtyard of the inn. His thoughts wandered back to this morning, and he smiled. The warmth of the coffee and conversation with Lian pulsed in his veins, and his body tensed with memory of what he had told her. "It's nice."

"Nice?" Paula raised her voice. "I thought you'd love it."

He released the curtain, and the backyard disappeared. Gripping the ledge of the sink, he stared at a spot on the granite counter and imagined coming home to this place day after day. The clip of Paula's sharp heels on the laminate flooring. The laughter of children in the backyard. The bark of a dog. His family. His home.

"Have you seen the bathrooms?" she asked. "They tiled the shower in the master bedroom and added a shower over tub in the hall bath for our future children."

He snapped his head in her direction. Our future children. Had she read his mind?

She clasped her hands together and widened her smile. Thank goodness she had not guessed his conflicted thoughts.

Following her lead, he strode across the carpet runners that dampened his footfalls on the hardwood floors. The house was quaintly furnished with plush couches, throw pillows, and antique furniture, but the modern touches reminded him of their soulless apartment.

In the master bathroom, he nodded at the tasteful tile in the shower stall. "How much are they asking?"

She stepped closer. "I think I can get them to accept under two million."

"*Under* two million?" he echoed. That amount was twice what he owed the bank on the inn's reverse mortgage. He sucked in a breath. "We don't qualify."

"Yes, we do," she said. "I talked to Joe, my mortgage broker, and he ran the preliminary numbers." She tapped her phone, bringing up his message. "Our mortgage payments would double from what we're paying in rent, but we'd get some of that money back during tax time since we'll be filing jointly once we're married."

"Double our rent?" He gaped. Where did she think they would come up with that extra income? "Are you expecting me to get a summer job to make up the difference?"

Frowning, she tossed her phone into her purse and crossed her arms over her chest. "We'll have extra money once the inn's sold. I figure after repaying the bank, the estate attorney, and any capital gains tax, you'll net enough to pay down the mortgage."

He raked a hand through his hair. Or they could avoid the capital gains tax if they moved into the inn. That's what his accountant told him after he inherited the property. He scrubbed a hand over his face. But that would mean he would have to find a way to refinance the reverse mortgage loan. How could he convince Paula to refinance with him?

"I don't know." He squeezed past her. If he had seen this place last week, he would have no doubts. Now, he thrust his hands into his pockets and strode around the rooms once more, taking everything into consideration. The property offered everything they needed. Old world charm and modern conveniences. A home office for Paula. And a third bedroom that had already been turned into a nursery. He sighed, leaning against the doorjamb of the baby's room.

Footsteps pattered behind him.

The familiar scent of her musky perfume triggered a memory. Something she said last night burrowed beneath his skin and festered like an infected splinter. He spun around and grabbed her wrists. "Why can't our future include our past?"

She pursed her lips, and her eyebrows pinched together. "What are you talking about?"

He shook her hands. "Why don't we pool our resources together and refinance the inn?"

Withdrawing her hands, she took a step back and laughed. "Seriously? I thought we'd already moved past the inn." She placed her hands on her hips. "Just because your grandparents were content to call that place home doesn't mean it's appropriate for our children." She shifted her weight and folded her arms over her chest. "For starters, there's no privacy."

"Yes, there is." He bunched his hands into fists. "The carriage house connects through a series of walkways from the courtyard. You can't see into the building from the main house."

She gestured behind her. "There's no yard for a swing set or a dog."

He rubbed his forehead. "You're right." He glanced up. "But there's a playground down the street."

She sneered. "Why would you want to walk our children down the street to play when we could have our own backyard?"

She was right. As usual. He sighed.

"I don't want to live at the inn," she said, lowering her voice. "That was never our plan." A glossy sheen covered her eyes. "We agreed on a house with a yard within walking distance to the elementary school." She held open her hands. "Why the change of heart?"

A flash from the diamond ring on her finger caught his attention. He flinched. That ring cost him a month's salary because his grandmother refused to give him her ring when he told her he wanted to propose to Paula. "She doesn't deserve you, sonny," Nana had said. "She'll always want more than you offer." Had Nana been right?

He dipped his chin to his chest and stared at his feet. "I don't know."

"What don't you know?"

Her sharp voice snapped against him.

Raising his head, he swallowed the tightness in his throat. "I don't know if I'm ready for marriage and a family." With you. He straightened his lips into a hard line.

"We've been together for five years. We're not getting any younger." She rubbed her nose with the back of a hand. "Why the cold feet?"

He toed the floor with his shoe. What excuse could he give her other than the truth? "We've been fighting a lot lately."

"Of course, we have." She threw open her arms. "Getting married and buying a house are two of the top ten stressors a couple can go through."

"Then maybe we should table them," he said. "Because I think mourning the deaths of loved ones is also in the top ten."

She grimaced. "You want us to miss out on this once in a lifetime opportunity because you haven't finished grieving?" She choked back tears. "I already agreed to push out the wedding till next year. Don't ask me to push out this house purchase too."

He ran a hand along his tense jaw. "Do we have to make a decision tonight?"

She folded her arms across her chest and pouted. "My clients gave us until tomorrow to decide."

"Then let's sleep on it," he said, gripping her shoulders. But he was only buying time.

Lian approached The Gables Inn with hesitancy. The afternoon breeze had settled into a mild spring day, but Lian shivered with the chill of betrayal. How could she write about a competing inn just to get back her old job?

Roman would never know, would he? She shuddered. Of course, she would tell him. She seemed to tell him anything and everything like she had given him front row seating to the inside of her mind.

But the access seemed to work both ways. Roman had told her about his indecision surrounding a future with Paula. Lian wasn't sure, but she would bet money he hadn't told anyone else. Not even Paula.

She strode toward the steps leading to the wrap-round porch. Her chest pinched. Maybe she should call Jaz and tell her she would pass on the opportunity to write this story, or any story, for that matter. She clutched her purse strap, but she didn't unzip the pocket and remove her phone.

After all, she was on vacation, and vacations meant not working.

She straightened her purse strap. She had been the one to reach out, not Jaz. What had she been hoping for?

A tug at the bottom of her stomach answered. Normalcy. She wanted to get back to the routine of her old life before her marriage imploded, before the pandemic, before everything she knew dematerialized.

Writing about travel had stabilized her. She could flit from location to location, an observer, detailing what others should come and experience. But she had never stepped into any particular place long enough to immerse herself in the reality of daily life. Those articles about the Caribbean islands talked about charm, not the legacy of wars and slavery. Even the tidbits on Europe didn't shine light on the employee strikes at the train stations or the lack of modern conveniences in the provinces. She only wrote what others wanted to see, not what she had witnessed, and that emptiness confronted her as she stood before the meticulously renovated Queen Anne with its white turrets, deep porches, and gingerbread trim all painted in the same deep green as the tiled roof. The building commandeered the street corner with its delusional self-importance.

Was her whole life one long escape? She took the first step up the flight of stairs. Was that why she had lost everything?

After pulling back the stained-glass door, she stepped into the comfort of luxury. She increased her stride across the modern lobby with faux pillars, gleaming wood counters, and recessed lighting. Tinkling piano music piped in through the sound system. Breathing in the fragrant air, she nodded at the vanilla candles strategically situated on polished side tables wedged between plush-looking sofas. The whole place looked staged.

At the reception desk, the staff wore matching suits with name tags pinned on their lapels. The quiet efficiency of the inn reminded her of the soulless chain-hotels she often stayed in when she wasn't writing on assignment.

"Are you here to check in?" a prim and polished young woman asked from behind the counter.

With a quick glance at the computer system, Lian shook her head. "No, I'm a reporter researching a story about literary locations for *Getaway* magazine. Is this inn inspired by the novel, *Anne of Green Gables*?"

The young woman handed her a brochure. "The Gables was built in 1888 and is owned by Boutique Hotels, LLC. The property was renovated four years ago. Each guest suite offers jetted tubs, fifty-inch flat screen TVs with state-of-the-art surround sound, premium coffee makers, refrigerators, microwaves, and complimentary Wi-Fi." She smiled. "We also have an elevator to the second floor and rooms that are compliant with the American Disabilities Act. Would you like to book a room?"

Lian spread the brochure on the counter and glanced at the glossy before and after photographs. Originally built twenty years before the publication of *Anne of Green Gables*, the building could not have been inspired by the quaint story of an orphaned girl adopted by two siblings needing help with their Prince Edward Island farm. "No, thank you." Lian slid the brochure across the counter and flashed a tight smile. "I appreciate you answering my question."

She dragged her feet across the threshold and escaped the suffocating atmosphere of luxurious convenience housed in a façade of history. Across the street, the ocean breeze returned, whipping her long hair across her eyes. With hunched shoulders, she strode back toward Valentino Inn.

After grabbing her phone from her purse, she called Jaz. "The story is a bust," she said. *Just like my life.* "It's just another corporate-owned inn. Nothing special." *Just like me.*

"Too bad," Jaz said. "How about any of the other B & B's?"

Lian stopped at the intersection, waiting for a car to pass. One disappointment after another took a toll on her mood and her self-esteem. For the last half of her career, she had chased superficial stories that meant nothing at the end of the day. Now, without a job or an assignment, she was free to discover a story that really mattered. She inhaled sharply, breathing in the briny air. "I think we should scrap this assignment."

"Are you sure?" Jaz asked.

"I'm positive."

"Okay, but if you change your mind, give me a call, okay? I really miss working with you."

"I miss working with you, too," Lian said, which was true. Working with Jaz was an ideal situation, a symbiosis of two minds that complemented each other. Lian straightened her shoulders. She couldn't spend the next four days researching the rest of the beds and breakfasts in the area in the hopes of finding a glamorous story for *Getaway* magazine. Not when she had something more important to investigate—herself.

Chapter Twelve

"Roman's not here," Rosa said, setting a silver tray full of bruschetta on the dining room table. "He doesn't usually come during the week. Between school and Paula, he's too busy."

"Of course," Lian said. A swoosh of heat flamed her face. She grabbed a plate and heaped it full of Italian meatballs, bruschetta, and mini flatbread pizzas and found a seat across from the picture window. She nibbled on the hot, savory appetizers, wondering why Roman had been here last night with Paula. Was it just to see her? She took a sip of the fizzy juice. What about this morning when he stopped by for coffee? She scrunched her forehead. Would he find a way to stop by tonight? Or should she stop hoping to see him?

"Good evening," John said, taking a seat beside her. He set his floppy hat on the table and ran a hand through his wispy white hair. "Mind if we join you?"

"No, of course, not." Lian flashed a smile. "How was your day?"

Jenn sat on the other side of her husband and leaned across the table. Her black hair matched her black-framed cat-eyed glasses, and her blue eyes crinkled at the corners when she smiled. "We had a wonderful time in Carmel."

Chuckling, John rolled his gaze upward. "She had fun. Shopping. I stood around holding her bags."

"You had fun, too." Jenn pointed a hand full of bruschetta at her husband and narrowed her eyes. "Don't tell me you didn't buy anything."

Leaning forward, John whispered, "I found a painting I liked."

"A Kinkade?" Lian asked. She met the artist once during a live demonstration during one of her travels.

"No, a little local artist who paints abstracts." He reached into his pocket and retrieved his phone. Scrolling through the pictures, he found what he wanted and showed her. "This little thing will go in our family room."

Lian gaped at the photo of Jenn standing beside a wall-sized gestural painting in fuchsia, turquoise, and yellow. "It's huge," she said. "How will you manage to get it home?"

"Oh, they'll ship it," John said.

"And they'll hang it, too," Jenn added.

Glancing at the elderly couple, Lian felt a pang of jealousy and regret over the loss of her own marriage. Once upon a time, happily ever after beckoned like a promise. Now the concept was some lofty goal only available for a chosen few. "Do you mind if I ask a personal question?"

John furrowed his leathery brow.

Jenn blinked her deep blue eyes and nodded.

"How do you manage to keep your love alive after all these years?" The question sounded trite, even in Lian's ears. But she scooted closer. Was there a secret?

Leaning back in the chair, John silently stared out the window. Slowly, he tapped his chin with a finger. "I don't know."

"We learned a lot from our first marriages," Jenn said, brushing crumbs from her fingertips. "We had no illusions. We were over fifty. We had stressful jobs and contentious exes and grown children who didn't want to talk to us anymore."

"So, we made a pact," John said, folding his lean arms over his chest. "We would retire early and see what we could of this world before we tired of one another."

"We didn't think we'd last more than five years, to be honest," Jenn said. She nudged John's shoulder and narrowed her gaze. "He's a cranky old man and I'm highly opinionated. We don't get along as well as it looks."

"But we learned to tolerate each other," John said. "Respect our differences."

"And keep our mouths shut." Jenn tugged an invisible zipper across her lips.

"And just enjoy the moment." John nodded toward the window overlooking the bay and smiled.

Lian gazed at the couple with new eyes. If she had not asked, she never would have known the years of struggle they endured together.

"And now look at us." Jenn curled her small hand around John's arm. "Thirty years and counting."

"We don't have a secret, dear," John said, squeezing Jenn's hand. "We just wake up and try our best."

Nodding, Lian absorbed their words like the roots of a plant. "I was married for a long time, and I thought the marriage was fine until it wasn't." Matt spent increasingly more time holed up in the home office programming while she sat in the family room writing her blog or cross-stitching in front of the TV.

"When did things go sour?" Jenn asked.

"During the pandemic," Lian said. "We were both at home, and we both kept to ourselves." She wiped her hands on her napkin. "Before that, I was traveling for business two to three weeks a month. Matt was at the office leading a software engineering team in product development at one of the big tech companies in Silicon Valley. We were always excited to see each other. We kept in touch by text and video calls."

"Sounds like you both were dating," John said, "rather than being an everyday couple."

Lian dabbed her lips with the napkin. Maybe John was right. The excitement of coming home after a few weeks on the road dissolved in the monotony of daily living.

"Don't worry about what's over," Jenn said. "Just enjoy your time here."

"I'm trying," Lian said. "But I've been a travel writer for as long as you both have been married. It's hard to just be someplace without thinking about how I can write about a location to make everyone want to visit."

John chuckled. "How can you write about this visit when the place you're staying is closing?"

"I can't."

"Then I guess Jenn's right. You'll just have to try and have fun," John said.

Fun. The word jogged a memory from this morning about Roman talking about his job teaching. *My whole life is fun.*

A wave of warmth moved through Lian's body, and she smiled. Maybe Roman could teach her how to make her whole life fun.

Roman carried the plastic bags full of Chinese takeout up the stairs to the apartment. The breeze had died down with the setting sun.

In the hallway, Paula fiddled with her key in the lock. "If we make an offer on that home, we won't have to deal with this mess." The bolt slid back, and the door swung open.

When had his relationship with Paula stopped being fun? He set the bags on the dining room table. Since the engagement last fall, everything had shifted from date night to deadlines. The wedding was scheduled for April, a year away, but already so much needed to be decided, from a venue to caterers to center pieces to music. The added stress of his grandparents' deaths and the complicated inheritance left him with little reserves for anything else. Viewing the house today shocked him into stunned silence.

After placing plates and silverware on the dining room table, he removed the takeout boxes, chopsticks, and napkins. Taking a seat across from Paula, he scooped out a mound of white rice and topped it with beef and broccoli.

Paula unloaded her briefcase onto the table. "I pulled up the comparison sales before I spoke with the sellers, so I know offering two million is fair." She slid the papers across the table and filled her plate with chicken chow mein.

He eyed the papers. "I thought you agreed we would sleep on it tonight."

Nodding, she pointed her chopsticks to the printouts. "I want you to review the comps to see if you agree with my offer."

"I trust your professional judgment." He nudged the pages toward her. "I need space to think about it. Okay?"

She twisted her lips as she chewed. A dribble of sauce splattered across her chin. He fought the impulse to reach across the table with a napkin and wipe it away.

"Roman?" She swallowed and rubbed a napkin over her lips.

His shoulders bristled. "If this is about the house, you need to drop it." His stomach clenched like his hand on the fork. The food didn't smell as good as it had in the restaurant.

"I think this home is perfect for us." She jutted her lower lip.

The pout would have softened his heart, if he could stop mulling over how she refused to help him refinance the inn. "Then you make an offer. By yourself." He tossed his napkin on the table. "I'm not ready."

"You'll *never* be ready," Paula yelled. "You'll always find some excuse to avoid responsibility."

"I don't like fighting," Roman said, standing. "My parents always fought until their divorce. Now they don't speak to each other. They won't even sit on the same side for our wedding." He choked on the words.

"We're not fighting," Paula said, lowering her voice. "We're discussing this opportunity." She gestured to the paperwork on the dining room table.

He frowned at the comparative market analysis. His grandparents had never discussed business while eating. They had taught him there was a time and place for everything. "I'm done talking," Roman said. "If you want to buy the place, then buy it. But I don't want to move forward with anything until the business I have with my grandparents is over." He held her gaze.

Paula's attention flickered to the calculator in her briefcase. She jabbed a finger against the keypad and frowned at the tiny screen. "The numbers don't work without your assistance. We need your income and your deposit."

"What deposit?" Roman didn't recall her mentioning a deposit.

Paula widened her eyes. "Well, I assumed you knew we would have to put twenty percent down to get an affordable mortgage. I figured you'd sell the inn for your share."

That tightness in his stomach cramped into a knot. "What if I don't want to sell?"

A dark shadow passed over her face. "The bank will take back the property."

The estate attorney had negotiated a six-month extension so Roman could refinance or sell. He still had two months left on that agreement. "Not if I can come up with another solution."

Paula gaped. "You signed the listing agreement."

"I can cancel the agreement in writing," Roman said.

"You know that's unwise," Paula said. "You could lose everything."

He paced back and forth beside the table. "Not if I find a way to refinance."

"You can't refinance." Paula scoffed, tossing back her head. "You didn't qualify for a loan."

"You're right." Roman stopped and faced her. "I don't qualify by myself. But if I can get someone else to go on the loan with me, I can save the inn."

Paula shook her head. "Who would refinance the inn with you?"

Roman narrowed his gaze. "Obviously, asking you is out of the question."

Dipping her head to her chest, Paula tapped her fingers against the table. "Roman, you need to be reasonable."

She spoke to him in a lowered voice like she was talking to a child. A flash of pain seared through his chest. "I am being reasonable. I want to wait to buy a home. You want to buy a home today. I already have a property I need to do something with as soon as possible. And you won't help me. So why should I help you?"

Sighing, Paula scooted her chair back and strode around the table to face him.

She reached for his hands, but he jerked them away to maintain his resolve.

"Roman, please." She clasped her hands to her chest. "Let's compromise."

"How?" He folded his arms and straightened his lips.

She glanced around the room before settling her gaze on his face. "We write the offer on the property and ask for a sixty-day close, which will give us time to sell the inn."

Shaking his head, he tightened his jaw. "You tell your clients we will pay full market value if they hold off listing the property for sixty days."

A dark laugh escaped her lips. "I don't believe you. Why pay full price?"

"Because I refuse to write an offer tonight." He dropped his arms to the sides and circled around her. Too bad if she didn't agree with his reasoning. He was done fighting.

"Where are you going?" Paula jogged after him.

He grabbed his backpack from the foyer and tossed it on the queen-sized mattress in the bedroom. He folded a pair of slacks and a dress shirt and tucked them into the backpack. After opening a chest of drawers, he selected T-shirts, socks, and underwear. "I thought I'd stay in my grandparents' house for tonight."

"Why?" Paula wriggled between him and the bed.

Roman tried to maneuver around her so he could retrieve his toiletries from the bathroom, but she darted from side to side. With his hands on his hips, he stopped and faced her. "Our relationship isn't fun anymore."

"Life isn't fun," Paula said, raising her arms to the sides. "But that doesn't mean you can just walk away."

"I'm not walking away. I'm leaving to get some space, okay?"

"No, it's not okay," Paula sobbed. "I don't want to lose the house."

Her lips trembled and her eyes glittered. She was crying about the house. A house without any family connection or memories. She was not crying about him. Or their relationship. Or what they could have in the future.

He struggled to breathe against the tightness in his chest.

A chasm opened between them.

She took a step forward.

Backing up, he refused to touch her. "You need that house," he said, stating a fact.

Sniffling, she rubbed her tear-streaked face with the back of her hand. Rivers of black mascara smeared on her cheeks. "I need you, too."

Between the tears and the softness of her voice, he wavered. But, deep down, the pit of his stomach remained clenched. If he gave into her tonight, what would he give into her tomorrow? And the day after that? Until the days stretched on forever, and none of his needs were ever met unless they matched her own.

"I love you," he said. "But I don't know if you love me or just the idea of getting married, having a family, and owning the perfect home."

"How can you even question how I feel?" She gulped. "Of course, I love you."

He searched for the truth in her face. "Then let me have my space."

"For how long?" she asked.

He couldn't answer. An urgency to flee the suffocating apartment and her incessant demands drove him to distraction. Had he packed his running clothes? What about his dress shoes? He wriggled past her and rifled through the contents of his backpack, silently listing off what he had and what he still needed. In the bathroom, he gathered his toothbrush, toothpaste, floss, and deodorant. What could he leave behind? Whatever the inn provided. Soap, shampoo, conditioner. He zipped up the backpack and slung it over his shoulder. "As long as it takes for me to sort things out."

"But what do I tell my clients?" She hovered beside him.

Her nearness prickled his nerves. "The truth."

She snickered. "That my fiancé has cold feet about the house?"

"No, you tell them we need time to settle a few outstanding items before we can make an offer." He strode past her through the living room to the front door.

"Roman?"

He gripped the doorknob as he looked back at her. She gaped, wide-eyed and slack mouthed, in the hallway. Sorrow pinched his chest, but he steeled his back. If he caved now, he would continue to give into her until he had nothing left of his own opinion. He would become his father, capitulating to his mother, until the love between them died. "Yes?"

Paula clasped and unclasped her hands. "What if I ask my parents to help with the finances until you decide what to do with the inn?"

Roman studied her jittery movements. "Fine. If that's how you feel, then do what you need to do. But leave me out of it." With one swift motion, he stepped outside and closed the door.

As soon as the front door slammed, Paula rushed to find her purse. In her haste to eat the Chinese takeout while discussing business, she had tossed her purse on the sofa in the living room. Rummaging through the pockets, she found her phone and speed-dialed her parents.

"Hello, sweetheart," her father said. "How's my girl?"

"Fine, Daddy." Paula sank into the comfort of the plush cushions, kicked off her shoes, and rubbed her tired feet. Her heartbeat still hammered from the fight with Roman. Why was he being so difficult, refusing to let go of his grandparents' inn and settling into the new life before them? She twirled a strand of hair and tucked it behind an ear. "Do you and Mom have a moment to discuss something?"

"Sure, sweetheart."

A patter of footsteps echoed across the line before her father returned and placed the phone on speaker.

"Hey, honey," her mother said in her sing-song voice. "Daddy says you have something you want to talk about."

"Yes, I do." Paula let her breath seep out. "Roman and I found the perfect starter home. My clients gave me forty-eight hours to write an offer before they list the property on the open market. But Roman isn't ready to commit until he sells his grandparents' inn, which will be going on the market next week." She tugged the ends of a strand of hair. "Since I don't want to lose this opportunity, I was wondering if you both had the ability to help with the deposit."

"How much, sweetheart?" her father asked.

"One hundred eighty thousand."

He whistled soft and low. "Are you sure this is the right house?"

"Positive." Paula tucked her feet under her hips and shifted the phone to her other ear. "Most starter homes are over two million in the area, and we'd be saving two hundred thousand by getting the home before a possible bidding war." She glanced up at the ceiling. "I've already spoken to Joe, our mortgage broker, so I know we qualify for the loan and the monthly payments. I just need help until Roman's ready with his half of the funds."

Her mother cleared her throat. "Honey, are you sure Roman will sell the inn? From what you've told us, he's pretty attached to that property."

Paula grumbled. "He *has* no choice. The inn hasn't broken even since the pandemic."

"What about his personal savings?" her father asked.

Paula scoffed. If the teacher's union didn't require contribution to a pension plan, Roman wouldn't have any money saved toward retirement. "He doesn't have that much," she confessed. The truth was he had a little over one hundred dollars from when he opened a savings account five years ago. Tension braided across her shoulders. Her parents didn't need to know that information. No need to alert them to Roman's lack of fiscal fitness. "He's a teacher," she said. "He earns next to nothing."

"I know buying your first home is tough," her mother said. "Your father and I spent ten years saving for a downpayment." She sighed. "Why don't you wait until you're *both* ready for this commitment?"

"We can't wait." Tears pricked her eyes. "We'll lose this house if we don't act by tomorrow."

"Don't cry, sweetheart," her father said. "We'll think of something."

Paula snuffled, rubbing a hand beneath her nose.

Her father hummed for a long moment. "Hey, I think I thought of something."

Paula straightened. "What?"

"Well, I'm not an attorney or a finance guy, so you might have to check to see if I'm right," her father said. "Your uncle Louie borrowed against his inheritance when his father died. Maybe Roman can borrow money from the estate. That way he can pay the estate back when the inn sells instead of paying us back."

Paula blinked. An inheritance loan. A slow smile spread across her face. "That's perfect, Daddy."

"Anything for my girl," her father said.

After ending the call with her parents, Paula uncurled her legs and stood. She dialed Roman, eager to share the good news. But the call went directly to voice mail. A buzz of panic vibrated through her body. She typed a quick text.

—*Call me. I have an idea that might get us the home.*—

Pacing the length of the soft carpet in her bare feet, she checked and rechecked the screen. But the phone didn't light up or ping with a response.

Hours later, when Paula still hadn't heard from Roman, she grabbed a jacket and shoved her feet into heels. Just as she was about to stalk over to the carriage house to tell him in person, her phone pinged.

—*Leave me out of it.*—

Dropping her hand from the front doorknob, she hitched her breath. How could she leave him out of the situation when he needed to apply for the inheritance loan to make the deal work? She shoved her keys into her purse and slid the strap high on her shoulder. Why was he being so unreasonable? Had she misinterpreted his message? Staring at the screen, she read the text again. A spike of anger jolted through her system. With trembling fingers, she typed with both hands.

—*What do you mean?*—

She bristled, waiting for some clarification of what to do next. Should she go to the carriage house anyway to talk to him in person? Or would he just refuse to open the door, leaving her cold and alone? She lingered in the hallway, breathing fast, her nerves a tangled mess. Finally, after what felt like forever, her phone chimed with a response. She gulped and swiped the screen to read his words.

—If you want the home, then buy it on your own.—

Exhaling, Paula slumped against the wall and slid to the cold tile floor. Maybe he misunderstood her request. Maybe she was being too pushy. Maybe, this. Maybe, that. Her head grew fuzzy with the possibilities. Determined to know the reason, she quickly typed.

—Why, Roman, why?—

Paula held the phone against her chest and waited. As the moments ticked by, and the room darkened, the phone remained silent.

Exhausted and defeated, Paula bowed her head and cried.

Chapter Thirteen

After responding to Paula's text, Roman turned off his phone and made up the bed in his grandparents' old bedroom. The room smelled musty, and he cranked open a window. The cool evening air, full of fog, floated into the room like a chilly breath. He turned on the hurricane lamps on each nightstand. The ghosts of the past lingered in the yellowed floral wallpaper and the four-poster bed. Even his reflection in the dual mirrors above the porcelain sink in the mahogany vanity in the far corner of the room resembled the image of his grandfather from the curtain of hair across his forehead to the slope of his nose to the pinch of his chin. He placed his clothes in the ancient armoire. When his grandparents died, one right after the other, he helped his father remove their personal belongings, including their photographs and clothes. Now, he sank down on the squeaky mattress and folded his hands between his knees. The weight of emptiness plunged through the center of him. How could he find comfort in the familiar surroundings when the people who had made this place a home no longer existed?

Grabbing his phone from his back pocket, he turned it on and called his father who had moved to Las Vegas after the divorce. A few years later, he had met and married his second wife, a cocktail waitress for one of the casinos. They had a child, a ten-year-old girl, named Mary, and Roman often wondered if his father had chosen the name because it reminded him of his mother.

"Hel-lo, sonny," Roman's father said. "What's cooking in your neck of the woods?"

Roman swallowed and clutched the phone tighter. "A lot, Dad." He steadied his voice. "Paula wants to buy a house before I've sold Pop and Nana's place. I don't know what to tell her. She won't listen to my concerns."

"And you thought I could help?" His father chuckled. "All your mom and I did was fight. And we didn't even fight fair."

Roman shifted his gaze to a spot on the checkered carpet. His grandparents had shielded him from most of those fights, keeping him here at the inn so he couldn't hear the worst of it. Maybe his father had changed his habits with his new family. He glanced up at the wallpaper and noticed a seam coming apart. "What about your new wife?" Roman had only met Terry once, at a wedding chapel in Las Vegas. He remembered she was younger than his father but older than him. He guessed she must be somewhere between forty and fifty by now. At the time, she seemed quiet and soft-spoken with dyed blonde hair and lots of makeup and a body that looked like it had a lot of work done. Nothing like his big, brassy mother with her fluffy brown hair. His mother used her big hips and big lips to her advantage—sashaying into a room and talking up a storm.

"Terry doesn't like to fight," his father said. "She's more likely to give in to whatever I say I want, which is a refreshing change from your mother."

Roman snickered, shifting the phone to his other ear. "Yeah, I know."

"Have you heard from her at all?" his father asked.

Why would his father ask about his mother? They hadn't spoken in years. Roman rubbed the stubble on his chin. "Mom still lives in San Diego with her sister, Aunt Izzy. We used to talk once a week, but she's been too busy to return my calls." Roman didn't mind. He never got along with his mother. She was always short-tempered and impatient, like she was in a hurry for him to grow up and leave so she could finally get on with her own life, which she had from what he could see. "I know she's okay because I follow her on social media. She has a fitness blog and sells protein bars and vitamins from an online store."

A moment of silence passed between them.

Roman stood and strode back and forth across the length of the room, his feet landing to avoid the creaky floorboard in the center of the room above the kitchen. When he was young, he always listened for that weak joist to cry out during Saturday mornings when he would get up early and sneak into the pantry for a bowl of sugary cereal before crossing through the pathways to the conference room at the inn where they kept the only TV on the property. He would sit and watch cartoons until the cereal bowl was empty, then he would cross back to the carriage house, wash the bowl, and return it to the cupboard and climb back into bed until the floorboard squeaked in his grandparents' bedroom. Then he would close his eyes and wait until someone knocked on his door so he could pretend he had just woken up. He smiled at the memory. Oh, how he missed those days.

"Dad, I'm calling because I don't want to sell the inn, and I'm wondering if you would help me refinance it."

"I'm sorry, sonny, but I'm on a fixed income now. I retired early when the doc said my heart wasn't good. Terry works two jobs to help us make ends meet." He cleared his throat. "Have you talked to Paula about helping out?"

"Yeah, I have." Roman moved aside the lace curtains and glanced out toward the coast. The fog was so thick, it swallowed the walking path. "She wants to sell the inn. I want to move into the carriage house and restore the inn. For Pop and Nana and me."

His father sighed. "I don't know what to tell you, sonny."

Roman dropped his shoulders, then hitched them again. "That's okay, Dad. I'm just glad you listened." He sat in a rocking chair and tipped back and forth, pushing off on the balls of his feet. "I guess I'll have to keep thinking of options."

"Or maybe it's time you let go," his father said. "You were always too attached to Nana and Pop. I know it was our fault. Your mom and I never paid you enough attention. We were too wrapped up in each other and fighting for what each of us wanted. You spent more time at that inn than you did at your own home. And, for that, I'm sorry."

"Don't be. I liked growing up with Nana and Pop." Warmth suffused his chest, and he smiled. His adoring grandparents taught him the beauty and power of teamwork in their efforts to make strangers feel at home while they were traveling far from home. The community his grandparents built gave him the security he needed to grow up with a sense of stability and responsibility for the greater good. That's why he taught elementary school. He wanted to give other kids the chance to experience what he had through sharing what he knew and showing them how life was full of opportunities for fun and excitement and learning.

"Well, sonny, I've got to go," his father said. "It's late, and I need to tuck Mary in and read her a story. You take care, and we'll talk later, okay?"

"Okay, thanks, Dad." A wistful smile played at the corner of Roman's lips. At least, his father's second child was receiving the benefits of the lessons he had learned while raising his first.

"I'll pray for you," his father said.

"Bye, Dad." Roman ended the call and stared at the empty space where his grandparents' crucifix had hung above the four-poster bed. When was the last time he had prayed? And would it help any if he started now?

In her room above the kitchen, Lian sat with her back propped against the pillows and her phone angled near her face for a video chat with her cousin, Geeta. She had called for advice about her stalled career, hoping Geeta might be able to lend some insight into the situation through her powers of intuition.

Through the tiny screen, Geeta shuffled a deck of tarot cards with her jeweled fingers. "Tell me when to stop," she said. The cards moved back and forth between her hands.

"Stop."

Geeta laid the cards down in a pattern on the table. She was about Lian's age, but her black hair was peppered with gray. With hazel eyes and a broad bone structure, she looked more like her German mother than her Chinese American father. Turning the first card over, she frowned. "Your problem is you've lost the youthful playfulness in your career."

"It's no longer fun," Lian agreed, hugging the otter to her chest.

The next card displayed a picture of a family sitting on a rainbow. Geeta smiled. "Your desire for a happy family will aid you on your journey."

Lian sneered. "What happy family? I'm divorced and childless."

"Your desire isn't dead," Geeta said.

A rush of heat infected her face, and Lian bit her lower lip to staunch a comment. She wasn't sure if she wanted to create her own family anymore, but she did miss living close to her relatives.

"Your past was full of inspired ideas," Geeta said, turning over another card. "But your immediate future shows you rejecting an offer…" Her voice trailed away.

Lian tilted the phone and frowned. "What's wrong?"

"I'm just a little confused," Geeta admitted. "The Knight of Cups reversed is usually about blocking the experience of true love, but we're talking about your career."

Lian laughed. "Well, the topic of my career might be considered true love. I did intend to write for *Getaway* magazine's destination wedding issue until the story went bust."

"Hmm…" Geeta rubbed her knuckles. "Well, let's see what the other cards say." She flipped over a picture of a man scrunching his face against a swarm of black crows circling his head. "You need to see the bigger picture beyond your current job loss. Maybe examine how you handle conflict and tension. Do you run away or confront things head-on?"

Ouch. A sharp pain lodged beneath Lian's breastbone. Whenever she fought with Matt, she always accepted the first assignment to an exotic location. She didn't stay around to work things out. Not an ideal quality to have in a personal relationship. But she never fought with her employer. "How does avoiding conflict affect my career?"

Geeta tilted her head. "Do you resolve differences with your employer or just move onto the next story?"

Lian puckered her lips, recalling her conversation with Jaz. "I don't need to argue with my editor over an assignment that doesn't exist," she said, thinking of the inn.

"Well, then, how do you explain your frustration and uncertainty?" Geeta asked, tapping the next card.

Lian wiggled against the pillows, trying to get comfortable but the lumpy mattress didn't help. "Maybe I need to find a new job."

"That might be true," Geeta said, showing her the next card. "You should explore all your options." She turned over another card and smiled. "Your current environment is conducive for exploring your full creative potential, but you're afraid of being alone." She flipped over the final card and gasped. "Your journey ends with a major decision."

"What major decision?" Lian frowned. "Am I offered two different jobs?"

Geeta shrugged. "I don't know anything about the details of this decision, only that it is a crossroads. One path will take you down one road, and the other path will take you on another, but you'll have to decide which path you want. You can't have it both ways."

Groaning, Lian propped her phone against a hurricane lamp and rubbed her temples. "This reading hasn't offered any clarity at all. Just more confusion."

Geeta laughed. "Well, dear, I suggest you sleep on it. Let what I said absorb into your dream space and maybe your subconscious will work things out for you."

"Easy for you to say," Lian said. "You've had the same job in the same town your whole life. You've never been lost."

A dark shadow flitted across Geeta's face as she gathered up the cards. "I may operate a spiritual shop in downtown Sebastopol, but I sometimes wonder if I closed myself off from more important opportunities."

"Like what?" Lian shifted against the pillows. She never imagined her cousin conflicted or confused.

"I used to work with the police department in missing persons cases, but I stopped once I failed to prevent the murder of my boyfriend's abducted niece." She tugged her lips into a straight line. "I sometimes wonder if my failure has prevented me from being more of service in this lifetime."

Lian swallowed. "I'm sorry to hear about that experience. How long ago did that happen?"

"Too long," Geeta said. She held Lian's gaze. "Just stay open and vigilant to any possibilities surrounding your career. You will be given a choice, and you need to choose wisely. Once a decision is made, you can't go back and undo it." She pursed her lips. "Just like I can't go back and work on missing persons cases anymore. That opportunity has passed. But I didn't just walk away from a career with law enforcement. I walked away from the love of my life. Ernie and I went our separate ways. We haven't seen each other in years."

"Oh, Geeta, I'm sorry." Lian squeezed the otter. "I'm sending you a big hug, and I promise to come up and visit after this vacation is over."

"One more thing, and then I'll let you go," Geeta said. "Whatever happens don't close your heart."

"What does my heart have to do with making a living?" Lian stood, shaking the pins and needles feeling from her legs. She grabbed the phone and paced beside the open window where harbor seals barked on the beach across the street.

"If you have a twinge in your gut, don't ignore it. Logic tends to lead us astray."

Lian groaned. "I thought talking with you would clarify things. But that tarot reading made everything more complicated. How am I supposed to be careful about making a life-changing decision without knowing what my options are?" She stopped pacing and broadened her stance. Glancing at the pink gerbera daisy in the crystal vase, she thought of Roman.

"The cards never lie," Geeta said. "If you need a step-by-step playbook, I suggest you go someplace quiet and listen until you hear your own voice speaking."

Lian ended the conversation more discouraged than before the call. Maybe she should have phoned one of her sisters instead. But she doubted her sisters would understand. Neither of them worked anymore. They were both stay-at-home moms with craft projects, homework assignments, and after school events. Grumbling, she tugged at the ends of her hair. At least, she could have listened to them complain about the hustle and bustle of their lives and feel a rush of gratitude at the simplicity of hers. She glanced at the digital clock across the bedroom and winced. Midnight. Too late to call either one of them now.

After getting ready for bed, she lay on the mattress and recounted her conversation with Geeta a dozen times. Her career indecision was impacting her entire life. And it shouldn't. She needed to give it a rest, not get hung up on ridiculous thoughts about some mysterious future opportunity that would change her life. But reason didn't help her fall asleep.

A snuffle rose from below. Tensing, she propped herself up on an elbow. Was someone here? Feet slapped and shuffled against the hardwood floors. Yes, someone was awake and wandering the inn. But who? The only other guests were the couple from Arizona. Lian couldn't imagine one half of the couple leaving the other half alone in the middle of the night.

Sitting upright, Lian sniffed. Did she smell homemade chocolate chip cookies? Lifting her chin, she wriggled her nose to confirm her suspicions. Yes, that sweet aroma seeped through the cracks of the floorboards and wrapped around her like a comforting hug. She tossed off the covers and let her feet sink into the soft carpet. Had Rosa returned to the inn to deliver dessert?

Or was Lian dreaming? Curious, she grabbed her room key and tiptoed down the stairs. The dimly lit lobby was empty. Following the scent, she ended up at the coffee station. Between the cream and sugar decanters, a stack of chocolate chip cookies lay on a silver platter. Snatching a cookie, she bit into the warm dough. Oh, heaven. Gooey streaks of chocolate smeared on her fingertips. She took another bite and closed her eyes, savoring the sweet warmth.

She grabbed a second cookie and wandered down the faintly lit hall, searching for Rosa to thank her for this small kindness.

From the conference room, a bright light beckoned.

She inched forward, her heartbeat lurching in her chest. The plush carpet swallowed the sound of her footsteps. Slowly, she poked her head into the open doorway, expecting to see Rosa. But the person sitting at the long table wasn't female. The fingers that gripped the yellow crayon were attached to a thick wrist and sinewy forearm. Squinting, she studied the graceful repetition of the person's hand. The waxy crayon tip scratched the surface of the paper. Transfixed by the rhythmic movement, her gaze lingered long after the person's identity snapped into focus.

"Roman?" she said.

At the sound of his name, Roman slammed the coloring book shut and lifted his chin. Heat prickled his face. Lian loomed in the doorway like a wavery apparition. His whole body nearly combusted in flames.

"I'm sorry," Lian said. "I didn't mean to disturb you."

"You just startled me," Roman said. Nodding, he gestured to the cookie in her hand and quirked his lips. "I see you found the cookies."

"I thought Rosa made these." Lian lifted her hand. "I was trying to find her to thank her."

"She didn't make them. I did." He motioned to the space beside him. "Care to join me?"

She stepped into the room. The long-sleeved pajama top and pants swallowed her slim figure. The overhead lighting illuminated a smattering of cookie crumbs on her upper lip. He ached to swipe his thumb across the surface before leaning over for a kiss, but he brushed aside those thoughts and cleared a space on the table instead.

"Thanks for the cookies." Lian sank into the chair beside him. "Hopefully, this midnight snack will help me sleep." Her gaze flitted to the closed coloring books and the mound of crayons on the other side of the table. Her eyebrows pinched together. "Speaking of sleep, shouldn't you be at home with Paula?"

Roman grabbed a thermos off the table and poured warm milk into the lid. He took a sip and offered it to her.

She dunked her cookie into the milk and took a bite. She widened her eyes. "Warm milk and cookies. You think of everything, don't you?"

He shrugged. "Like you, I couldn't sleep." He glanced at the coloring book and crayons. Lian hadn't been insulting or dismissive about him being here in the middle of the night coloring like an errant child. He took another sip of warm milk and dropped his original plan of defensive avoidance to confess the truth. "Paula and I aren't getting along right now, so I decided to stay at the carriage house until things settle down between us." He gestured toward the coloring books and crayons. "I made the cookies and warmed the milk and came here to relax." He waved a hand around the room. "When I was a kid, I would sneak down here on Saturday mornings to watch TV and eat cold cereal. During the week, I would do my homework at this table and color afterward. This room always brought me peace."

Lian licked her lips, clearing the crumbs and leaving a trail of glistening moisture. "What's on your mind?" She finished the cookie and dusted her hands together. After taking a sip of warm milk, she settled back against the chair. "I'm worried about my career options. But why are you and Paula fighting?" She arched an eyebrow. "Or is that just a habit you guys have?"

He smirked. "If it's a habit, it's a bad one." He folded his arms on the table and leaned toward her. She seemed so fragile and tiny, from her glossy black hair to her bare feet. Even the rosebuds printed on her pajamas seemed vulnerable. "We looked at a house. Technically, it's perfect for us. Three bedrooms, two bathrooms, a big yard, and walking distance to my work." He sighed. "Paula wanted to write an offer right away. I wanted to sleep on it. We couldn't agree, so we ended up in a fight." He gestured to her. "What about you? Why are you concerned about your career?"

Lian dropped her gaze. "I don't know what I'm going to do with my life after this vacation is over." She folded her hands in her lap. "The pandemic changed everything. My marriage failed. My career ended." She glanced at him.

"My whole sense of self has been shaken up. I don't know who I am or what I want anymore."

Gazing at her, Roman nodded. "I felt the same way after my grandparents died." He bowed his head, staring at the swirls of wood grain on the table. "At first, I wanted to get rid of everything. I boxed my grandparents' belongings and stowed them in the attic. But the longer I worked with the estate attorney, the more I realized I didn't want to give up this place." He released his arms and leaned back against the chair, staring around the conference room. "The inn is my childhood." After opening his backpack, he gathered the crayons. "I talked to my father tonight, hoping he could help me brainstorm a way to keep this place, but he told me maybe it's time I let go and move on with my life."

Lian touched his elbow. "Are you leaving?"

The frisson of her soft touch radiated up his arm and filled him with warmth. He stopped moving. It was late. He should go. "Do you want me to stay?"

Nodding, Lian pointed toward the coloring books. "Mind if I color with you?"

Roman lifted his eyebrows and studied her. No adult had ever asked to color with him.

"I've heard it's supposed to be relaxing," Lian said.

"It is." Roman removed the crayons he had stuffed into his backpack and handed her one of the coloring books. "I'm sorry I only have superheroes and monster trucks," he said. "I wasn't expecting a girl to join me."

Lian snickered. "I don't mind monster trucks." She opened the coloring book and pointed to the black and white pictures. "I always envied my sisters because they shared one coloring book while I had one of my own. I should have been grateful for the luxury of not sharing, but I was jealous of their intimacy. Even after all these years, I still feel left out. They're both married with children and living their best lives while I'm divorced and childless wondering what to do with my life."

The loneliness in her voice echoed in his body. Offering a handful of crayons, he nodded to the open pages. "Why don't we share this coloring book? I'll take this side, and you take the other. Okay?"

Lian met his gaze. "Okay."

Her pupils were so large and dark, they made her eyes look black. Her small voice swelled with hope. He scooted his chair closer and grabbed a red crayon to shade the panels of the truck. "We're having career day at school tomorrow. Or technically, today. You should come. The kids are so imaginative. They might give you some ideas."

"Really?"

"Yes." He glanced over at her. The edges of his body blurred.

"Okay." She nodded and smiled. "I'll come."

"Great." A sense of relief washed over him. "I'll give you details before you go."

"Thanks." With a steady hand, she traced the outline of a tire with a black crayon. "I have some ideas on how to save the inn, but I think you should talk to Paula first."

Tension braided down his back. Why did he always have to consult with Paula? She wasn't the boss of him, was she? "I'll text her tomorrow before I leave for school."

"Sounds good." She dipped her head and focused on the task of staying within the lines. The skin between her eyebrows pinched and the creases around her mouth deepened.

A few strands of her long hair caressed his arm. A rush of energy ricocheted throughout his body. Awake and alert, he nudged a little closer. A gentle heat rose from her skin. He leaned toward her until he was almost touching, so close, too close, and yet a whole world away.

Chapter Fourteen

Twenty pairs of eyes stared at Lian. She stood next to Roman before his classroom of six-year-old children. Why had she agreed to this visit? Last night while coloring with Roman the thought of being with children for an hour sounded fun. Now, standing with a frozen smile and stiff legs, she doubted her decision.

"Class, we have a special visitor today." Roman took a step forward. "Please welcome my friend, Lian Shu." Smiling, he gestured to Lian.

The students cheered. "Welcome, Lian."

Roman widened his smile. "Lian is here today because she's looking for ideas on what to do now that she's finished working as a travel writer. Let's see if we can help her by reading the book *When I Grow Up*." He plucked the picture book from his desk and held it up so everyone could see. Taking a step back, he nudged Lian's elbow. "Why don't you pull my chair around and have a seat?"

Nodding, Lian scampered to Roman's desk and wheeled his chair around to the nearest table of first graders. She sat and dumped her purse beside her legs.

A couple of students scooted toward the outer edges of the table, making room for her. Those same children stared at her with wide eyes and gaping mouths.

What were they thinking? Her breath eased out of her nose. Relax. They won't bite. She smiled and nodded.

The children snapped their mouths closed and glanced away.

Mimicking the children, Lian folded her hands in her lap and swiveled her attention toward the front of the classroom.

Still standing, Roman opened the book and read about a boy who wondered if he should be a gorilla masseuse or an artist who sculpted with chocolate mousse when he grew up.

The children burst into laughter as each potential job grew more and more outrageous.

Lian softened her clasped hands in her lap. Smiling, giggling faces surrounded her. Tightness loosened from her chest. Why not be a pickle inspector or a movie director? Or a rodeo clown riding upside down? She grinned.

"Now I want you to think about what you want to be when you grow up," Roman said, passing the picture book around so the students could examine the illustrations more closely. "We're going to draw pictures of our ideas and share them."

Walking from table to table, Roman placed a white sheet of paper before each student along with a box of crayons. He winked when he handed a set to Lian. "Do your best," he said. "Let your imagination go wild."

With trembling fingers, Lian accepted the paper and crayons.

Beside her, a boy scribbled a picture of a man holding a long hose. Water gushed in an arc. "I want to be a firefighter like my daddy when I grow up," he said.

The girl beside him drew a picture of a ballerina. "I'm going to be a famous dancer," she said.

"What do you like to do?" a tiny voice asked.

Lian gazed into the dark eyes of the girl sitting across from her. "I...I...don't know." Her mind was as blank as her sheet of paper.

"Why don't you know what you like to do?" the girl asked.

"I don't know," Lian repeated. She wiggled in the seat, glancing over her shoulder.

Roman wandered around the other side of the classroom. He nodded and smiled. Every now and then, he bent to speak to a student.

Sighing, she turned back to the students at her table.

"You know what you like to do," the boy who wanted to be a firefighter said. "You're just scared to tell us because we might laugh." The boy stopped drawing and glanced at the students sitting around the table. "Let's promise we won't laugh."

"We promise," the students said in unison.

"Okay," the boy who wanted to be a firefighter said, "go ahead and tell us."

Lian gazed into his serious blue eyes and gulped. How could she convince this table full of children she honestly didn't know what she liked anymore? She scrunched her face, trying to think back to when she was six years old. But her mind froze. What had she enjoyed as a kid?

After what felt like a lifetime, a torn and faded memory emerged. Lian sat cross-legged in front of the television with her younger sisters listening to Shirley Temple in *Bright Eyes*. Her lips curled into a smile. "I liked to sing," she said, straightening her back.

The table of students cheered.

"Sing for us," the blue-eyed boy commanded.

Lian cleared her throat and opened her mouth releasing the words to the song, "On the Good Ship Lollipop."

After the first few discordant notes, the blue-eyed boy wrinkled his nose.

The girl beside him covered her ears.

And the children across from them clapped their hands over their mouths.

Lian immediately stopped singing. Heat raged over her skin, and she scrubbed her hands over her face. "I guess I'm not a good singer," she said.

The blue-eyed boy shrugged. "Maybe you'd sound better if you touched your toes."

"Or wiggled your nose," the girl beside him suggested.

"Or smelled a rose," the girl across from Lian said.

Before Lian could respond, the bell rang to announce recess.

The students yelped. A flurry of arms shoved crayons into boxes and stacked pictures into neat piles. A blaze of feet scrambled to line up in single file before the door. As soon as Roman propped the door open, the children tumbled onto the playground like dandelions blown by the wind. Their hoots and hollers bounced across the blacktop and echoed back into the emptied room.

"Let's go," Roman said, ushering Lian out of the classroom. "I have yard duty."

Lian grabbed her purse from the floor and followed him out to the playground. The wind whipped her hair across her face, and she tried to tuck the errant strands behind her ears.

"What did you think?" Roman asked, crossing the blacktop.

"Of the kids, or the occupations?" Lian asked, trailing beside him.

"Both." He stopped beneath the branches of a budding tree, held her gaze, and smiled.

Lian stood beside him, staring into his bright and hopeful face. He really did believe in unlimited possibilities. Too bad she didn't share his perspective. She scrunched her shoulders at the memory of her awful singing voice and the kindness of the children who did not laugh. "The kids are kids. They don't know about real life." She shrugged and scanned the playground. "Not everyone can make a living doing what they like to do because they might not be suited for the work. Like me and my singing." She tipped back her head, and a dark laugh escaped from her lips. "I do appreciate the effort. But I don't think I have a knack for anything other than what I've been doing." She tugged her arms across her body. "Maybe I should go."

"You can't leave without saying goodbye," Roman said. "They're kids. They need closure." He touched her elbow. "Just wait until after recess. Then we'll share the drawings, and you can tell them all about travel writing." He dropped his arm and waited.

The heat from his fingertips imprinted on her skin. She swayed on her feet, suddenly lightheaded.

Biting her lower lip, she focused on his suggestion. A little adult perspective for the children wouldn't hurt, would it? She could talk about the glamorous things she once loved about the job—the foreign sights, smells, sounds, and tastes of different cultures and their foods—and omit the things she hated—the rampant poverty outside the resorts, the hostile politics of some nations, and the cities that weren't safe for women to travel alone.

She stared at Roman's expectant face. Oh, why did he always manage to wrangle her away from her better judgment?

"Okay." She nodded. "I'll stay."

After recess, the students filed back into the classroom and took their seats. Roman asked for volunteers to share their pictures and explain their occupations. Once the students finished, Roman led Lian back to the front of the classroom. With her hands tightly clasped in front of her ramrod body, she looked more like a woman sentenced to death than an adult facing a classroom of six-year-olds.

"Relax," he said, jostling her arm. "You'll do fine." Turning to the class, he smiled. "It's your turn to ask Lian any questions about being a travel writer." He squeezed her elbow once, then took a seat behind his desk.

Across the room, Jeremy raised his hand. He was the oldest member of the class, and he was the most outspoken.

"Yes," Lian said. "What's your question?"

"Did you travel around the world?" Jeremy smiled and sat back down with a heavy *thunk* against the plastic chair.

"Yes," Lian said. "I've been to 192 countries since I graduated from college."

Aside from her nerves, Lian seemed like a natural.

Another hand shot up. Natasha straightened her spine and her lips. Roman never tired of her serious posture. He imagined she might grow up to be a leader someday.

Lian nodded.

"Did you visit Africa?" Natasha asked.

"Yes, I went to Tanzania to try out the safaris," Lian said. "The magazine I worked for wanted to know which one was the best, so I got to try several safaris in the area and write up my reviews on each of them."

Timmy in the back waved his hand. "Did you see lions?"

"How about tigers?"

Roman interjected. "One question at a time, please. And remember to wait until Lian calls you."

The room hushed.

The same student who spoke out of turn raised a hand. "And bears?"

Roman glowered. "You didn't wait to be called."

Lian snickered. "I did see lions and tigers." She shifted her weight to one foot, gazing at the student who spoke out of turn. "But I saw bears in Yosemite during another trip for a different article."

Chara, a girl with pigtails, raised her hand.

"Yes," Lian said, nodding toward her.

"How many articles did you write?" Chara asked.

Lian gazed up at the ceiling, silently moving her lips. Lowering her gaze, she chuckled. "Too many to count."

Frowning, Miguel lifted his hand. "Why do you want to be someone else now?"

Tipping her head to the side, Lian gnawed her lower lip. The stiffness returned to her posture.

Roman shifted forward in his seat. Should he intervene?

Breathing deeply, Lian clasped and unclasped her hands. She frowned, and her eyebrows pinched together. "The pandemic changed me. I used to be on the road constantly. Three years of not going anywhere forced me to look at the one place I had never been—home."

Roman gulped. Home. She was getting personal. Maybe too personal with the children.

His phone pinged from his desk. He frowned. Did he forget to turn it off? He tapped the screen and read the message.

—Can we talk about the house?—

Paula. He clenched his jaw. If he didn't respond, she would blow up his phone with messages. Quickly, he typed.

—Meet you at the apartment at 2:30 today.—

Without waiting for a response, he silenced the ringer and tossed the phone back on the desk. Sighing, he scanned the room. What had he missed?

Lian showed the class the picture she drew of musical notes. "I wanted to be a singer, but I don't have a good voice." She smiled. "Does anyone have another suggestion?"

That's it. Roman crossed one loafered foot against his knee. Turn the focus back on the students.

A quarter of the class raised their hands.

Lian pointed to each student, one after another, and fielded the answers.

"Have you tried being a doctor?"

"Or a librarian?"

"How about a dog trainer?"

"A bus driver."

"A vet."

"A garbage collector."

"A mail carrier."

"How about a chef?"

"An airplane pilot."

"A mommy."

Lian blinked. "Those are all good suggestions." Her voice wavered, and her eyes glistened.

Oh, no. Roman untangled his legs and stood, circling to the front of the classroom. Please, don't cry. Placing a hand against her shoulder blades, he rubbed her back just like he did whenever a student ran up to him after falling and scraping their knees on the playground.

She stood like a statue beside him.

No amount of kneading eased the tension in her back. He stopped massaging and wrapped his arm around her shoulders, tucking her into his side. "Class, our time is up."

The students groaned.

"I know, it's sad, but Lian needs to go." He smiled, rubbing her shoulder. "Let's thank Lian for her time."

"Thank you, Lian," the students said.

He steered her toward the back door. "Will you be all right?"

She nodded. "I think so."

He squeezed her shoulder and lowered his voice. "They didn't mean to mention motherhood."

"I know." She strained a smile. "They're kids. They don't know any better."

He dropped his hand and stepped back. "How does six-thirty sound for dinner?"

She frowned. "Aren't you meeting Paula to talk about the house?"

Paula. Again. He sucked his teeth and ran a hand through his hair. "We're talking after school. I should be free for dinner."

She bit her lower lip and glanced over his shoulder. "You better get back to your students. They're restless."

He opened his arms for a hug. "Only if you agree to dinner."

Folding him close, she squeezed. "I don't want to take you away from your fiancée. You've got a lot to discuss."

Closing his eyes, he breathed in the floral scent of her shampoo. How could he get her to change her mind?

The students jeered. "Lian and Mr. Valentino, sitting in a tree, h-u-g-g-i-n-g."

He laughed, snapping open his eyes and letting go. He spun around and clapped his hands. "Okay, class, let's get ready for math."

But the students continued singing. "First comes love, then comes marriage, then comes—"

"Enough, class." He held up a hand, cutting them off before they could sing, "a baby in a baby carriage."

The door clicked shut. He glanced over his shoulder, and a sharp pain shot across his chest.

Lian was gone.

Chapter Fifteen

At two-thirty, Paula unlocked the door to the apartment. Silence echoed in the hallway. A quick glance at the empty abalone shell on the table confirmed Roman wasn't home. She kicked off her heels and strode to the living room to wait. She had an evening appointment with another pair of sellers who would be reviewing the two offers she had received today on their home. Sinking into the plush sofa, she typed.

—Where are you?—

Cupping the phone in her hands, she leaned forward with her elbows on her thighs and stared at the tiny screen. The same dread she felt when she told her clients she would not be writing an offer on her dream home returned, creeping up her back and settling on her shoulders. Closing her eyes, she tried to block out the look of disappointment reflected in the wife's gaze and the quizzical expression on the husband's face.

"I thought you and your fiancé wanted to move here," the husband said.

"We do," Paula stammered. "But we can't do anything until his grandparents' property sells, which could be next week or next month or longer."

The wife tugged on her husband's shirt sleeve. "Why don't we accept a contingent offer?"

He shrugged off her hand and frowned. "We can't if we want to close on our new home, remember?"

At that point, the baby cried, and the wife left.

Alone with the husband, Paula tried her best to maintain her composure. She didn't want her clients to know she felt more for the home than what the property was worth.

Now, her phone pinged with a message, and she tapped the screen to read it.

—*Sorry. Last minute conversation with a parent. Leaving now.*—

Paula sighed, tossed the phone on the coffee table, and wandered into the kitchen for a glass of water. Roman always said she worked too much, but he wasn't any better. He treated the students as if they were his own children, arriving early and staying late and discussing progress and problems with their parents whenever needed.

By the time the key jangled in the lock, Paula braced for a confrontation. But Roman swept into the apartment, all arms and legs like an excited puppy. He shrugged off his backpack as he strode into the kitchen where Paula sat drinking a second glass of iced water.

"Sorry I'm late," he said, tossing the backpack onto a chair. "Tasha's parents wanted to know how she was doing with reading, and I lost track of the time." He grabbed a glass from the cupboard and filled it with water from the tap. Taking a seat next to her, he gulped a few swallows before setting the glass on a coaster. "How was your day?"

Paula tapped her fingers against the glass. How dare he act like nothing happened after he stormed out of their apartment last night? She sucked in a breath. "It's not over yet. I have offers to present at six-thirty." She tugged her lips into a straight line. "You'll have to eat dinner without me."

"Okay." He shrugged.

That's it? She pushed back her shoulders. "I had to tell my clients we wouldn't be writing an offer. I think the wife felt sorry for me." She cut her gaze toward him. He stared at her with wide-eyed innocence. The muscles in her jaw tensed. "So, I guess we'll just have to wait till after the inn sells before we buy anything, right?"

Roman dipped his head toward his chin and traced the sides of the glass with a finger. "Actually, I'm not selling the inn."

Tipping back her head, Paula laughed. "Are you delusional? How many times do I have to go over the facts?" She narrowed her gaze. "You have no other option unless you want the bank to take back the property."

"Actually, I have a call into the estate attorney to discuss selling off as many assets as possible."

Grumbling, she shook her head. "I added up the totals from the appraisals."

He pursed his lips. "Appraisals are just estimates. They don't tell you what people will pay on the open market, especially if you're dealing with zealous collectors."

"Zealous collectors?" She gaped. "Who wants to buy tarnished silver and early American artwork?" She slapped her forehead. "Oh, that's right. I forgot about the junk in the garage between that rusted Model T and the broken pinball machine. All that crap must be worth a million dollars."

He grimaced. "I'll find a way." Leaning back against the chair, he swept an arm across the room. "I'm moving back to the inn to save expenses. You're welcome to join me."

"In the carriage house?" She scoffed, folding her arms over her chest. "Are you crazy?" She shot a glance around the modern kitchen with stainless-steel appliances, recessed lighting, and dual pane windows. How did he expect her to live in a run-down shack with dated appliances, old-fashioned lamps, and casement windows?

"Then I guess I'll come visit you," Roman said, pushing back his chair and standing. "I'll send you my half of the rent to cover this month, but next month you're on your own."

"Seriously?" She towered beside him. "You're moving out?"

Nodding, he brushed past her.

She caught his arm before he exited.

He tugged against her clenched fist.

"Wait." Her voice quivered. "Maybe we can find another solution."

Spinning out of her grasp, he glowered. "You want that home. I want the inn." His nostrils flared. "Don't you see? We aren't on the same page anymore."

She thumped a fist against her open palm. "We *were* on the same page. Just last week. What happened?"

He placed his hands on his hips and broadened his stance. "When you knew I wouldn't qualify for a loan on my own, why didn't you apply with me?"

She took a step back. "Because that place has always come between us."

He kept his gaze level. "*That place* or my grandparents?" He twisted his lips and blinked a few times. "I know Nana and Pop didn't like you, but I never let their opinion influence our relationship."

She nodded. "You're right." Nana had refused to give him her engagement ring when he wanted to propose. She thought Paula was too pushy. But Roman didn't care what Nana thought. He went ahead and purchased a ring on his own. Paula glanced at the tiny sparkle on her finger and shuddered. She had wanted a larger diamond, but Roman had wanted a smaller price tag. They had settled on a half carat solitaire. Staring at the gemstone, Paula thought the compromise was reasonable. But when she shared her ring with her girlfriends, they all laughed. "The larger the stone, the bigger the love," they said, sporting their one carat diamond rings. And when Roman told his guy friends how much he spent, they all speculated Paula's tastes were too big for his budget. She twisted the ring on her finger. Would marrying only lead to more sacrifices and compromises that would fester into a lifetime of bitterness and resentment?

Pacing, he raked his fingers through his hair. "We're becoming my parents, and we aren't even married yet." His voice broke, and he turned away, his shoulders shaking.

Oh, great. She winced. Another crying jag. When would the grieving end? A prickle of awareness dawned at the outskirts of her mind. She didn't have to wait for Roman to recover from the loss. She had other options. After wriggling the ring off her finger, she tapped his shoulder.

He turned around.

"I'm done." She plunged the ring into his hand. "We're over."

"We're what?" He widened his eyes.

"Over. Done. Finished." She didn't know how many other words he needed to hear to understand their relationship had ended. "You don't need a wife. You're already married to the inn." Stalking into the living room, she sank into the nearest sofa and buried her head in her hands. "I don't want us to end up like your parents—divorced after having kids." Tears pricked her eyes. "I should have known it was over when you said you had to think about making an offer on what should have been our dream home." She exhaled and let the tension slump off her shoulders.

The cushions shifted beside her, and a warm weight draped across her back. "I'm sorry," Roman whispered, as he stroked her hair.

Slowly, Paula lifted her head and sniffled. Pain welled up behind her eyes. She touched the rough stubble on his cheek for the last time. "I'm sorry, too," she said.

Chapter Sixteen

After fleeing the school, Lian drove past the inn toward the coast. The windy 17-mile drive cut along the edge of the peninsula past rocky beaches with crashing waves and rolling golf courses and historic landmarks, from lighthouses to cypress trees. She didn't stop to appreciate any of these locations. Her hands gripped the steering wheel tightly, the window rolled down to let the sharp wind slap her face.

In Carmel, she parked and walked up and down the iconic streets dotted with quaint boutique shops and one-of-a-kind restaurants. Again, she powered through the place, marching in her sneakered feet, up and down the hilly roads, never stopping. She could have been anywhere, doing anything. But she was here, in a tourist town, running away from the one thing she couldn't escape—herself.

Now, after the exhausting late morning and early afternoon, she ended up back in Monterey, straight to Cannery Row and the open arms of the aquarium where she sat on a bench facing the penguin exhibit, waiting for the three-thirty feeding to start.

A cluster of children plastered their hands against the glass. Their parents and guardians stood behind them like sentinels keeping watch. The chatter of their voices rose and fell like ocean waves, crashing against Lian's ears. She cringed, but she did not move away from the excitement.

Over a loudspeaker, a volunteer announced the feeding would be starting shortly. From a brochure, Lian read that April and May encompassed the mating season. The same penguins would pair up for life, creating a new family each year. The male and the female penguins would take turns warming the eggs in the nests built into the rocky caves. While one sat, the other hunted, bringing fish to the mate.

When the feeding started, the volunteers flung fish at both the waddling penguins on the craggy platform and their mates sitting on eggs in the caverns. One penguin brought its fish to its mate in the cave and offered it. The sitting penguin pecked at the fish before handing it back to its partner.

Lian hitched her breath. How romantic. Even when the volunteers met the birds' needs, the instinct to feed and care for one's mate remained.

"Hey, Lian."

Her heartbeat lurched in her chest, and she jerked her head in the direction of the voice.

A tall man wearing a floppy hat waved. A small woman with cat-eyed glasses wandered next to him.

Exhaling, she relaxed her shoulders and smiled. "John and Jenn." She scooted down the bench, making room for them to sit. "You're just in time for the last feeding."

John tipped back his hat and scratched his head. "Actually, we're on our way to the theater to watch a movie about Luna, the otter they found on the beach."

"I'm a sucker for a tear-jerker," Jenn said, patting John's arm.

Staring at the couple, Lian's face warmed against the memory of Roman's broad hand nestled in her lower back as she stood before the classroom of children.

"Would you like to join us?" John asked.

Lian shook her head. "I'll stay and watch the penguins."

Arm-in-arm, John and Jenn left.

Lian propped her elbows on her knees and cradled her chin in her hands. Would she ever find someone who would make her feel both secure and loved? Matt had been financially stable, able to keep down a job and a home, but he hadn't been able to anchor her to that home or a life together. She sighed, watching the penguins. Maybe she was doomed to wander. Whenever she traveled, she never felt lost. Until now.

When the feeding ended, the wall of people dispersed. Parents pushed strollers. Toddlers clutched their parent's hands. Children hopped, skipped, and jumped to the next exhibit. Their laughter receded, leaving Lian sitting alone on the bench.

Blinking away the moisture in her eyes, Lian thought. About all those IVF treatments. She hunched her shoulders. About all those years of being disappointed month after month. She bit her lip. About all the time she avoided her sisters because their families reminded her of everything she did not have. She hitched her breath. About all the children in Roman's classroom, giving her career suggestions, including motherhood. She buried her face in her hands. All that pain swelled within her again, and she braced against the grief that never seemed to end.

From her purse, her phone rang.

She jumped at the familiar sound. Rummaging through the pockets, she found the phone and swiped the screen. "Hello."

"Lian, it's Jaz."

"Hi, Jaz." Lian smiled. A small zip of energy pumped through her. Jaz only called when she had good news.

"We just got a story I can't find anyone to cover," Jaz said. "It's three months in Eastern Europe to revitalize the tourist industry. With the war in Ukraine, no one wants to go there. We need someone who can write good promotional materials. Can you leave next week after your vacation?"

Lian glanced at the penguins toddling along the craggy platform. If she went to Eastern Europe, she could avoid the loneliness of her Campbell apartment. "I guess."

"Great. We'll fly you out next Tuesday. I'll send details by email."

"Wait." Her heartbeat stuttered in her chest. "Are you offering me a job?"

"An assignment. Not a job." Jaz paused. "But it's a step in the right direction, isn't it?"

"Maybe. Maybe not." Lian straightened her spine. She didn't need to respond with that same knee-jerk reaction of fleeing her life whenever things got tough. She could wait. See what other opportunities surfaced. Just like Geeta had told her last night. "I need to think about it."

"Don't think too long. I need an answer by Friday."

Tomorrow? A zip of panic flooded her system. She pushed a strand of hair away from her face. Be strong. She didn't need to cave to pressure. She could control the pace of her life, and not anyone else. "That's too soon. Can you give me till Monday?"

"You're pushing your luck," Jaz said. "But I'm almost certain you'll take it, so I'll give you the weekend to think about it."

"Thanks." Lian hung up, stunned. Just a day ago, she believed her career was over. Now another chance had sprung up.

Grabbing her purse, Lian tossed her phone inside and slung the strap over her shoulder. Walking toward the nearest exit, she passed families milling about exhibits of underwater life. Lightness ballooned in her chest. She could travel again and escape the suffocating intimacy of her life. Queasiness fluttered in her stomach. Or she could turn down the assignment and tackle the obstacles that she constantly avoided in her life.

Roman shifted the box against his hip and jostled the knob to the front door of the carriage house. The door swung open, and he stepped inside. After flicking on the lights, he set the box on the coffee table in the parlor and went back to his car to retrieve the other boxes. When he finished, he shut the front door and glanced around the gloomy luminescence. His back ached, and his stomach grumbled. In his hurry to pack up his belongings, he neglected to eat or drink anything.

From his back pocket, his phone rang.

A knot of tension braided across his shoulders. He checked the screen and blew out a breath. The estate attorney had finally called.

Roman swiped the screen. "Sheridan," he said. "Thanks for returning my call."

"Sorry it's late," Sheridan said. "I've been swamped. Seems like death doesn't stop for spring." He choked on a bitter laugh.

Roman scooted aside another box from the sofa and perched on the edge of the velvet cushions. "So, I have some news. I want to keep the inn. I need your help to brainstorm how we can make that happen."

Sheridan whistled, soft and low. "We already went through all the options with Paula."

"Paula's no longer in the picture," Roman said, trying his best to stabilize his voice. "We ended our relationship today, and I've moved into the inn. That's why I need to keep the place."

"I'm sorry to hear about your broken engagement."

"Well, it's all for the best." Roman sighed. "We weren't getting along anymore." He glanced around the room with its antique lamps and furniture. "How much do you think I can get for Pop's 1918 Ford Model T car?"

"Not much. It needs to be restored. Maybe twenty-five thousand."

"How about the pool table and the old juke box?" Roman asked. "I know the pinball machine is broken, but what about the victrola record player?"

Sheridan heaved a sigh. "Those items are listed on the appraisal. If I remember correctly, they total well under the amount needed to repay the loan." He paused. "I'm sorry to hear your personal situation has changed, but my professional opinion remains the same. Go ahead and sell the inn. Then you can walk away with a little cash and start a new life."

A new life. He grumbled. Without a fiancée. Or an apartment. He raked his fingers through his hair. At least, he had a job.

"Okay, well, I appreciate your candor," Roman said, sagging against the cushions.

"I wish I had better advice for you," Sheridan said. "You know I cared deeply about your grandparents, and I hate the idea of selling that place as much as you do. But facts are facts."

As soon as Roman ended the call, he flung the phone onto the coffee table. He lurched to his feet, pacing the length of the parlor. Through the French doors, the muted early evening light slanted across the carpet runner and the scuffed hardwood floors. He grumbled, his thoughts tumbling in his mind. He had to think of something.

Wait. He froze. Didn't Lian say she had some ideas?

He checked the time. Seven o'clock. His stomach churned again. Hopefully, she hadn't eaten either. Grabbing his phone off the coffee table, he sent a text.

—*Dinner?*—

A few moments later, his phone chimed.

—*How did the talk go?*—

He sucked in a breath. His fingers trembled as he typed.

—*Not good. We broke up. I spent the afternoon moving into the carriage house. I'm tired and hungry. Have you eaten?*—

He slumped on the sofa and stared at the fairy lights draped across the courtyard. Too bad he couldn't see into the inn. Was Lian there?

His phone pinged.

—*Sorry about your broken engagement. Not in the mood to eat.*—

A tingle rippled across his scalp. Was she upset over what happened in the classroom today?

—*Did the kids get to you?*—

He sat on the sofa, trying to get comfortable. But doubt and fear immobilized his muscles. If he couldn't pay off the loan in two months, he would lose the inn to the bank. He would be left with the antiques, and no home.

His phone chimed, and he swept his finger across the screen.

—*No. The kids were fine. Not sure about a job possibility. That's all.*—

Good. He nodded. At least, the kids hadn't spooked her with their rendition of "Sitting in a Tree."

—*What's the job possibility?*—

—*Eastern Europe. Three months. Leave next week.*—

—*Why won't you take it?*—

—*Not sure if it's right.*—

He didn't know what was right either. He tapped his phone against his palm, thinking.

He had been wrong about so many things. When he was moving his boxes into the carriage house, he finally saw the problems Paula had mentioned, which he had ignored. The wallpaper was peeling in a few of the rooms. The faucet in the downstairs bathroom dripped. All the appliances in the kitchen were dated. Even if he could find a way to keep the property, he needed money to fix it up.

Frowning, he scratched an itch on his chin. Maybe his father was right, too. He should let the place go. A muscle twitched in his jaw. Every time he thought about the inn no longer existing, he imagined his whole childhood gone.

After a long moment of staring at nothing, he sent another text.

—*You said you had some ideas on how to save this place. Maybe we can discuss over drinks.*—

A few seconds later, his phone pinged.

—*I don't drink.*—

He chuckled.

—*Me, either. But maybe we should start.*—

He added a smiley face.

A few seconds later, she responded with a laughing-till-tears-stream-down-your-cheeks face and another message.

—*Okay. We can go to dinner. It might be good to talk.*—

He smiled and typed.

—*I'll meet you in the lobby of the inn in ten minutes.*—

—*Okay. See you soon.*—

He stood and tucked the phone in his back pocket. His muscles still ached, but a renewed energy propelled him forward.

He was meeting Lian for dinner.

Chapter Seventeen

Lian gasped at the view from the Beach House deck. The sun dipped close to the horizon, casting gold, rose, and orange rays across the gentle waves lapping Lovers Point Beach and the Monterey Peninsula. Taking a seat beside a patio heater, she fixed her gaze on the surroundings. Couples and families gathered at tables glowing with the firefly light of tea candles. The scent of buttery seafood mingled with the salty sea breeze.

The hostess set two menus on the table.

Lian unrolled the silverware and tucked the napkin in her lap. Raising her head, she glanced into Roman's large brown eyes. The intensity of his gaze plummeted through her body, and she smiled. In all her years of travel, she always looked across the table at empty space. Roman's warm and inviting gaze rooted her. Her smile widened. "I hope the food is as good as the view."

Roman tucked the white napkin in his lap and gestured to the menu. "I recommend ordering from the specials. They're always a hit with both tourists and locals."

"I'm not hungry," she said. But all around her, the scent of grilled fish and crisp fries and chocolate cake wafted in the air. A low tug pulled at the bottom of her stomach. She opened the menu and scanned the offerings.

"Get something, and whatever you don't eat, I'll take it with me for lunch tomorrow," he said. "It'll save me from having to pack a sandwich, and I'll be the envy of all the teachers in the lunchroom."

"Okay." She dipped her head and read. Every now and then, she glanced over at him. In the candlelight, the lines on his forehead and the shadows beneath his eyes were more pronounced. He must be dead tired from staying up late last night and working a full day with the students.

A server approached the table. "Would you like to order a bottle of wine or something from the bar?" he asked.

"Oh, no, thanks," Lian said. "I'll stick with water."

"Me, too," Roman said. "But you may tell us about tonight's specials."

The server smiled, showing a line of straight teeth. "We have the lobster roll and the fisherman's platter. The lobster roll is a ciabatta bun filled with fresh lobster tails and served with a side of coleslaw or our homemade fries. And our fisherman's platter features the fresh catch of the day, seasoned shrimp, prawns, and scallops and comes with steamed vegetables and wild rice." He bowed. "I'll be back with your waters."

Roman closed his menu. "I'm getting the fisherman's platter. How about you?"

"The lobster roll sounds good," Lian said.

"Perfect," Roman said. "I'm looking forward to lunch tomorrow." He winked.

A low-grade heat radiated up her chest and into her face. She swallowed and glanced away, twirling the napkin in her hands. The patrons around them were dressed in T-shirts and shorts. But Roman wore slacks and a button-up shirt with sleeves rolled up above the wrists. His dark hair gleamed from a recent shower, and when the breeze blew, a whiff of his fresh-smelling aftershave tickled her nose. If she didn't know any better, she might have mistaken tonight's dinner for a date.

The server delivered their glasses of water and took their orders and returned with a basket full of bread and butter.

Roman tore off a slice of bread from the half-loaf. "So, tell me about your ideas on how to save the inn."

"Have you considered refinancing?" She buttered a piece of warm bread.

He nodded, and a dark cloud passed over his face. "Already tried that avenue."

"What happened?" She arched an eyebrow. Refinancing was the simplest solution. That's what she and Matt did during the divorce, so Matt had the cash to pay her half of the home's equity.

"I don't qualify on my own." He ran his fingers up and down the sides of the water glass, then widened his eyes. "Would you consider partnering with me?"

"Partnering?" She touched her chest with her fingertips. "I know nothing about the hospitality business. I've always been on the receiving end."

He chuckled. "You wouldn't have to work at the inn. You'd be an investor on the loan."

"Oh." She wiped her fingers on the napkin. "I'm not sure how loans work, but I'm pretty sure you need an income. I only have assets from the divorce."

He groaned. "Okay, so that's out." He leaned against the table. "So, what's the next idea?"

She shrugged. "I stopped researching options once you told me you were selling to buy a place with Paula."

He flinched.

The hurt was visible on his face. "I'm sorry I mentioned her."

"No, don't be." He waved his hand, but a muscle twitched in his jaw. "She was a big part of my life for five years, and it's too bad things ended." He twisted his lips. "But it's probably all for the best. We'd been fighting for a long time, and it was only getting worse."

"You're right. It's better to end things now than after you're married," she said. "Divorce isn't easy."

"Well, I'll take your word on that one." He took a sip of water and glanced at the ocean.

A glassy, faraway look danced in his eyes. She shivered. What was he thinking? She bit her lip and navigated her thoughts back toward the conversation. "How much do you owe on the inn?"

He blinked, shifting his gaze toward her. "One million."

"Yikes," she sputtered. The knife slipped out of her hand and clanked against the bread plate.

"I know it's a lot," he said, picking up the knife and handing it back to her. "The worst part is I only have two months left before the bank will take back the property."

She tucked the knife next to the plate and almost choked on a mouthful of bread and butter. He just broke up with his fiancée and moved into the carriage house. "Where will you go if you lose the inn?"

"I don't know." He pushed aside his bread plate and folded his arms on the table. "I'll probably ask around. Maybe another teacher has a room I can rent until I find a more permanent solution." He slumped his shoulders. "I'm more worried about the staff being unemployed."

She sucked in a breath. "Have you considered crowdfunding?"

He furrowed his brow. "You mean going online and asking strangers for donations?"

"Not strangers." She winced. That phrase sounded harsh and impersonal. She relaxed her shoulders. "Friends of the inn."

He chuckled.

"I'm serious," she said. "A singer once crowdfunded a million dollars to produce a record. If she can do it, you can do it."

"I wouldn't know where to start." He leaned back and crossed his arms over his chest. "In spite of being part of the tech generation, I'm woefully behind when it comes to that stuff." He arched an eyebrow. "I'm much more comfortable with paper and crayons."

She laughed. "You do color a mean monster truck."

The server cleared the empty breadbasket and brought their entrées.

"Okay, your turn," he said, digging into the fisherman's platter. "Tell me about this job offer."

"It's not a job offer. It's an assignment." She explained the difference. "I'm torn because I'm not sure if I want to travel anymore." She paused, holding the ciabatta bun in both hands. Her gaze wandered over the dark waves, and her thoughts floated away.

"Why don't you want to travel?" he asked. "I thought you missed it."

"I did," she said, drawing her gaze back to the table. "But that was before my marriage ended."

"Travel killed your marriage?" He scrunched his face, and his eyebrows pinched together.

"No, not exactly." She took a bite of the crunchy bun and sweet, meaty lobster tails. Mmm. The food here was good. She swallowed. "I think I used travel as an excuse to avoid conflict and intimacy."

"Oh," he said, nodding. "If you're not home, you don't have to deal with it."

"Exactly."

He held her gaze a moment longer. "You don't have to travel to avoid your problems," he said. "You can stay right here and bury your head in the sand."

"Like you?" She teased, grabbing a fry off her plate.

"I admit I've been negligent in the past, but not anymore."

"Mm-hm," she said, gnawing on a crispy potato. "What's changed?"

A flicker of light danced across his eyes before he glanced away. "So, if you don't accept this assignment, what will you do?"

"You can't answer a question with another question," she said.

He quirked his lips into a smile. "If you like to avoid trouble and can't travel, you can."

"Touché." She let her mind drift amongst the light and shadows along the beach and the ocean. The sky had darkened, and the beginnings of fog rolled off the horizon. She tilted her head to the side and smiled. "What a beautiful night. I wish I could stay here forever."

"Then stay," he said.

The words sounded like an invitation. She turned toward him, studying the solemn look on his face. A world of possibilities opened. What did she have to go back to? An empty apartment, a job she didn't have anymore, and no immediate family or friends to buffer daily life. But the prospect of moving here, or anywhere for that matter, dug up deep fears. She laughed, fiddling with her silverware. "You make it sound so easy."

"It is." He reached across the table and touched her wrist.

A spark triggered an instinctive reaction, and she tucked her hand into her lap. His fingertips had branded her skin.

"You could stay at the inn, as a permanent resident," he said, his gaze flickering from where her hand had been. "If I lose the inn, then we could move someplace else."

"Together?" The prospect of living with Roman rushed at her like a huge wave.

He shrugged, sitting back, retreating. "It's an option."

She twirled the napkin in her hands. If Roman could find a way to keep the inn, then this opportunity of staying in one place might work. Lian could become a local but surround herself with strangers who would drift in and out of her life. Oh, sure, some guests would return on a regular basis like John and Jenn, but most of the people she would meet would only be passing by. She wouldn't have to open her heart up to everyone. She could pick and choose, pulling some close and keeping others far away.

The server stopped by and refilled their glasses of water. "Everything okay?" he asked.

Roman nodded.

Lian smiled, her focus on Roman. "It's perfect," she said.

After dinner and dessert, Roman paid the check, stood, and held out his hand. "Ready to go?"

Lian languished against the chair like a cat beneath a ray of sunlight. She groaned. "Can we stay a little bit longer? I don't think I can walk."

"Don't worry," he said. "I can carry you. Just grab the to-go bag and hop onto my back."

She narrowed her gaze. "I weigh more than I look."

"And I'm stronger than I look." He flexed both arms, posing like a body builder.

She giggled and stood. "Okay, we'll leave." She grabbed the to-go bag and shuffled ahead of him across the deck toward the stairwell.

With a quick swooping glance, he took in her black hair, bare shoulders, and dainty feet. Zigzagging back up, his gaze lingered on the sway of her hips in the form-fitting sundress.

At the bottom of the staircase, he nodded toward the paved path that cut across the waterfront. The night was beautiful, all shades of silver and blue, with a resounding silence broken only by the shuffle of their feet.

He didn't want to break the magic spell. So much of tonight had been wonderful, even if it hadn't solved either of their problems. He still didn't know if or how he could rescue the inn, and she expressed she didn't know whether to accept this new assignment or find another direction for her life. The uncertainty shifted something hard inside him, breaking into fissures, and threatening to slide into the pit of his stomach. The air stilled, and the cold fog pulled back, leaving a quiet clarity. A buzzing thrummed through his body. When the feeling swirled into a dizzying chaos, he touched her elbow. "May I ask you a question?"

She stopped, glancing down at his fingers on her forearm. "Sure."

He breathed in deeply to steady his nerves, but when he spoke his voice quavered. "Why did it take you so long to come back?"

She turned to look up at him. A frown pinched her softly glowing face. "What do you mean?"

Shuffling his feet back and forth across the sandy path, he studied her face. In the peek-a-boo moonlight, her almond-shaped eyes glowed like incandescent fog. He swallowed against the tightness in his throat. "Before you left, you promised you'd return. Why did it take you a lifetime to come back?"

She raised her eyebrows, and her eyes widened like smokey orbs. She shifted the bag from one hand to the other and dipped her head to her chest. The dark crown of her head gleamed like black satin. "I shouldn't have made that promise," she said. Her voice was soft and low. "I never intended to come back." She met his gaze. "All my assignments are one-offs."

One-offs. He bit his lip to staunch the pain welling up inside of him. All this time he believed in her promise. But the statement had been a pretty lie to pacify him. The truth stung. "Tell me why you returned."

"I already told you. I wanted to find myself." She pivoted and started walking. "Why ask again?"

He stumbled forward to catch up with her pace. The urgency to confide everything rushed from the center of him and spewed out of his mouth. "I had the biggest crush on you when we first met. I kept telling Nana you would come back for me, and she told me I was being foolish. So, when I saw you at the inn and you recognized me, I took it as a sign."

"A sign?" She halted and spun. Her mouth gaped like a black hole. "Are you saying you've carried a torch for me all these years? Is that why you broke up with Paula? So, you could live out your childhood fantasy of being with me?"

The words flung like rocks against his head. He dodged but they hit him anyway. "I didn't break up with Paula. *She* broke up with *me*." But even he could tell the semantics didn't make much difference.

Sighing, she stalked toward the wooden railing and glowered at the cypress trees on the rocky cliffs then down at the dark water.

He crept up beside her, leaving a foot or two of space between them for safety, and folded his arms against the railing. "I'm sorry." The words felt flat and heavy against his tongue. A deep shame spread like a rash across his body. Nana was right. He had been stupid to believe Lian meant what she said. But he was a child who trusted miracles. And seeing her again after all those years just confirmed his desire. Dreams did come true. Until they ended up being a coincidence.

"Don't be," she said, cutting her gaze toward him. "I should be apologizing to you." She glanced back at the beach where harbor seals slept, their bodies tucked close to one another. "I have a confession to make." She paused. Lifting her head, she met his gaze. "Remember that picture you drew for me? I hung it on my fridge. Every time Matt asked if he could remove it, I refused. Over the years, the edges curled, and the crayon faded, but I kept it right there where I could see it every day." She inhaled sharply. "I must have misplaced it when I moved out of the house because I haven't been able to find it since the divorce."

He uncurled from the railing and took a step closer. Hope bloomed in his chest. "Why did you keep it?"

She shrugged, and the to-go bag rustled against her thigh. "I had so much fun that week." She smiled. "You were so adorable. I taught you how to read, and you taught me how to play. The picture reminded me of the trip, and how happy I had been."

"When was the last time you were happy?" He sidled up to her, only inches apart. If he moved any closer, he would skim against her.

She lifted her gaze toward the sky. "Last night when we were coloring together." She tilted her head. "How about you? When was the last time you were happy?"

He grasped her bare shoulders with his broad hands and turned her to face him. "Right now." He dipped his head and brushed his lips against her mouth. She shivered. The tension in her shoulders slackened, and the to-go bag dropped between her feet. She parted her lips and darted her tongue into his mouth. He moaned. She tasted sweet and salty. He slid his hands down her arms and grasped her fingers.

When the kiss ended, he touched his forehead to the top of her head and sighed. "That was wonderful."

"Mm-hm," she said.

The fog rolled back toward them, and she shuddered.

"Are you cold?" He untangled his fingers and rubbed his hands up and down the length of her cool arms.

She nodded, shifting closer.

The heat from their bodies vibrated like a shimmering wall between them.

He closed the distance, folding his arms around her back. The warmth of her body crushed against him, and he closed his eyes, soaking in the feel of her curves.

She wove her fingers into his hair. Her mouth nibbled his earlobe before nipping at the tender skin of his neck.

A rush of heat powered through him, and he clutched her tight against a swoon of dizziness. How far was the inn? Would they ever make it back? Or would they stay forever rooted to the trail above the beach?

She broke away, first. "We should get back." Her breath heaved from her chest.

"You're right." He ran his hands down his stomach, smoothing out the creases on his shirt. "It's late and a school night."

Nodding, she picked up the to-go bag and started walking again.

After shoving his hands into his pockets, he matched her stride.

At the juncture, he offered to carry the to-go bag.

"No," she said, swinging the bag between them. "You paid for dinner. The least I can do is carry the leftovers home."

Home. He placed his hand on her lower back as they crossed the street. The lights in the inn glowed above the parking lot. At the base of the staircase, he paused. "So, does that mean you're moving here?"

She twisted her lips and shrugged. "I'll think about it."

The noncommittal answer rubbed against his ribs. "Don't think too long," he said. "I don't want you talking yourself out of the right decision."

She laughed. "How do you know me so well so soon?"

He wove his fingers through hers and led her up the stairs to the inn's front door. "Because I've been thinking about you for years." He unlocked the door and held it open for her. "Goodnight, Lian."

She handed him the to-go bag. "Will I find you in the conference room coloring at midnight?"

Chuckling, he took the bag from her hand. "I hope not. I need my sleep."

She hovered on the doorstep, glancing at the lights in the lobby then back up into his eyes. "I'm tired too, but I doubt I'll sleep."

He raked his fingers through his hair. "I'll leave the coloring books and crayons in the conference room."

"What if I don't want to color alone?"

A muscle twitched in his jaw. Was this her idea of an invitation for something more?

Before he could ask, she grabbed his free hand and pulled him closer.

He inhaled sharply, feeling a quake of energy rumble through his body. A fierce, dangerous heat emanated from her skin. He swallowed and blinked, staring at her slightly parted lips. Leaning down, he brushed his mouth against hers.

She released his hand and wrapped her arms around his neck and pressed her body against him.

Nudging apart her lips with his tongue, he dipped inside the cavern of her mouth. She tasted like dessert. He dropped the to-go bag beside his feet and twisted his hands into her hair, breathing in the fragrance of her honeysuckle shampoo. She was so slight and cool against the flame of his body.

Gasping, she pulled away. "Come to my room."

"Are you sure?" He cupped his hands against her lower back and studied her face. Her lips were swollen, and her eyes were half-closed. "I don't want you to regret anything."

"I won't."

"Are you positive?" Fear loomed like a shadow beside him. "I just broke up with Paula. You're still healing from a divorce." He sighed. "Maybe we should wait."

"Why wait?" she asked. "It's Thursday night. I leave Sunday morning."

His breath hitched. How could he make love to her tonight only to let her go a few days from now? Shaking his head, he slid his hands up her back. "I don't want one night."

"We can't always get what we want. Why not take what we need?" She raked her fingers across his chest.

A tingling sensation rippled throughout his body, making his legs weak. Swallowing, he tangled his fingers through her hair. Leaning into her, he breathed in the floral scent of her shampoo and closed his eyes. How could he turn down this opportunity?

His thoughts spiraled back to childhood when he longed for a train set. He didn't want to wait for his birthday, but he didn't have the money to buy it immediately. When he asked Pop to loan him the money, Pop told him, "Some things are better if you wait." At the time, he pouted and pined for that coveted train set. But when he finally got it, weeks later, after earning enough money from extra chores, he cherished that train set more than he did any other of his toys. Because he earned it. He wanted to earn Lian's love, even if he couldn't do it in the next three days.

With a finger, he tipped her chin toward him so he could gaze into her eyes. "Believe me, I want to make love to you more than anything in the world." He swallowed, and his throat burned. "But I can't."

The disappointment reflected in her eyes pierced his chest. He held her hands, cold and limp against his palms, and tried to reassure her. "I don't want a fling. I want a relationship. Do you understand?"

For a long moment, he waited.

Finally, she bobbed her chin. "It doesn't make me happy, but I think I understand."

Her voice was weak and small. He wrapped his arms around her and held her close, never wanting to let go.

Chapter Eighteen

Lian turned the skeleton key in the lock to her room, flicked on the switch, and closed the door. Golden light diffused against the faded wallpaper and cast shadows against the hardwood floor. After tossing her purse on the table between the rocking chairs, she collapsed on her back against the lumpy mattress. How had she failed to seduce a guy who had been crushing on her since childhood? She cupped her hands over her face and grumbled. What type of loser was she?

All her failures seemed to dance around her. Being born a girl, and not a boy. Graduating in the middle of her class, and not at the top. Marrying a programmer, and not a business owner. Being childless, even with medical assistance. Divorcing said programmer, instead of working things out. Losing her job, and not finding a new one.

She rolled onto her side and hugged a pillow, letting the tears squeeze out of her tired eyes.

Memories of the night floated through her mind like flotsam and jetsam. The view from the deck. The foggy sky. The inky ocean. The sleeping harbor seals. The fire of Roman's hand on her elbow. His lips gently caressing her mouth. The briny taste of his strong tongue in her mouth. His hand cupping her lower back. His voice, soft and low. The hunger in his big brown eyes. The way his hair fell over his forehead when he said, "I don't want a fling. I want a relationship."

Flopping onto her back, she groaned. How would she get to sleep tonight when all she could think about was Roman? Every inch of her body itched with a furious need for a fling, something quick and meaningless. Not a relationship. A relationship meant work and commitment and staying in one place long enough for anything to matter.

Sure, she had considered staying in Pacific Grove. But she always imagined it as a home base, a place where she could keep her belongings while she traveled the world. If she wanted to put roots anywhere, did she want to do it in the inn with the guy who wanted more than she could give?

Glancing at the digital clock, she read the time. Just before eleven. Too late to call anyone, even Geeta.

Determined to forget about this latest failure, she brushed her teeth and changed into her pajamas. Lying beneath the covers, she turned off the lights. Outside the casement windows, the waves lapped at the beach across the street. Should she stay or should she go? The plush otter rubbed against her, and she hugged it tight against her chest.

Restless and awake, she let her thoughts drift to last night. Coloring next to Roman in the conference room had lulled her into a hypnotic state. Something about the movement of wax scratching against paper soothed her.

After an hour, she slipped out of bed, grabbed her key from the nightstand, and left the room. She padded down the staircase to the lobby and wandered down the lighted hall to the conference room. Gulping, she placed a hand on the cold doorknob. She steeled her back against disappointment. But with one twist, the door opened. Exhaling, she stepped inside and flicked on the light.

The room illuminated with a soft glow, from the floral wallpaper to the paisley rugs on the hardwood floor. The long conference table that dominated the room faced the big screen TV. As promised, a stack of coloring books and crayons sat in a corner of the table.

Lian pulled back a chair and sank into the soft cushion. She opened the first book. With her thumb and index finger, she flipped through the pages until she found the ones colored from last night. Her heartbeat ticked in her chest. On her page, every image was carefully outlined in crayon and shaded with even strokes. On his page, the colors came from all angles and often spilled outside the lines. With the pad of her finger, she traced the crazy waxy pattern. *He's an original. A yin to my yang.* Her lips curled into a smile.

After turning to a new page, she picked up a red crayon. Without first tracing the outline of the fire truck, she started shading, letting the color smear all over the image, without a care in the world.

She colored one truck after another until her eyes grew heavy and her thoughts stilled.

At six, an alarm bleeped. Roman reached over the pillow and switched off the annoying sound before he rolled over onto his side. But he couldn't drift back to sleep. He punched the extra pillow, staring at the cold, empty space beside him. If he had accepted Lian's invitation last night, he would have woken up with her long dark hair spilled against his shoulder and her almond-shaped eyes blinking in the faint light.

Why had he turned her away?

An ache of loneliness squeezed his chest. Time for a run. If he finished early, he could look at the appraisal and see if there was anything the estate attorney and Paula might have missed. He also needed to pay the bills. Groaning, he scooted out of the warm bed and strode out of the room, careful to skip the squeaky floorboard. He descended the staircase in his bare feet. A chill rose all around him in the silent house.

In the kitchen, he started a pot of coffee and grabbed his workout clothes from where he left them draped over the back of the sofa in the parlor. Once dressed, he laced up his shoes and left.

The cool air filled his lungs as he pumped his arms back and forth, lengthening his stride as he ran past his old apartment and across the street to the sandy trail that he and Lian had walked last night. In the blush of sunrise, the tops of the houses glowed fluorescent pink as luminescent as the purple ice plants blooming along the trail. Passing other early morning joggers, he raced ahead, keeping his eyes focused on the peak of Lovers Point.

Running usually cleared his mind, but this morning everything he passed reminded him of Lian—the railing where she stood looking out at the dark ocean, the sandy trail where her sandaled feet shuffled, the stretch of pavement that wound up the back steps of the Beach House where her hips swayed beneath her sundress.

Minutes later, when he reached the top of the lookout, he stood on the rocky summit and scanned the view. He breathed in the briny air and swiped the sweat off his forehead. In the distance, harbor seals barked. Sea gulls swooped and cried. And dark waves swished, heaping seaweed on the shore.

From the pinnacle, he squinted. Valentino Inn was just a pink dot in the distance. He could not tell if Lian's light was on, or if her curtains were drawn.

Did she sleep last night? Or had she spent wakeful hours coloring in the conference room?

He placed his hands on his hips and drew in a deep breath of salty air. His chest pinched. Maybe he should have invited her to sleep at the carriage house last night.

No, that thought would have been a bad idea. A knot twisted in his stomach. He had fallen for her once already, as a child. He didn't need to torture himself with her presence now that he was a man.

A gust of wind rushed up his spine, and he shuddered. Turning, he jogged down the craggy rocks and jumped back on the trail retracing his steps to the carriage house.

Breathless and sweaty, he flung open the kitchen door and poured a cup of coffee. He stirred in some creamer and collapsed in a hard wooden chair at the table. Taking a sip, he listened to the achy silence of the empty building.

His grandparents were gone.

Paula was gone.

And Lian might be leaving, come Sunday.

He gulped a mouthful of coffee. The heat seared the back of his throat and burned the lining of his stomach.

Without the people he loved, this place was no longer home.

Chapter Nineteen

After breakfast, Lian sat in the dining room watching the marine layer burn off the coast while drinking a second cup of coffee. She had slept well after a half hour of coloring in the conference room. She still didn't know whether to accept *Getaway* magazine's travel assignment to Eastern Europe or find work someplace else or whether to relocate to Pacific Grove or stay in her Bay Area apartment, but she no longer worried about those decisions. Today she planned on enjoying each moment before her vacation dwindled away.

A commotion of bumping and banging jostled her out of her relaxed state, and she shifted in her chair. Jenn fluttered into the dining room, glancing from one end to the other. "Where's Rosa?"

"In the kitchen," Lian said. Jenn looked flushed and worried with her forehead crinkled and her mouth downturned. "What's wrong?"

John bounded into the dining room, dragging a suitcase behind him. "Jenn's daughter has gone into labor a week early. We're leaving now and wanted to take something to eat."

The swinging door to the kitchen opened, and Rosa bustled into the room. "I'll pack up something. You just wait a few minutes."

"Thank you." Jenn sank into the nearest chair and scrubbed a hand across her forehead. "We'll probably miss the birth. She's already dilated five centimeters."

John parked the suitcase beside the table and massaged his hands against Jenn's shoulders. "Now, now, don't worry. We got the first flight out."

Grumbling, Jenn shook her head. "A lot can happen in two hours."

Rosa emerged from the kitchen, holding a cardboard box. "Toast, hard boiled eggs, granola, and fruit cups," she said. "Nothing messy."

"Thank you." John cradled the box in his arms. "We appreciate it. I'm sorry to leave early." He glanced around the room and blinked several times. "I can't believe this place won't be here next year."

Lian touched her fingers to her chest. "Actually, Roman's trying to save the inn," she said. "He needs a million dollars to pay off the loan, but he has a couple of months to figure it out."

"One million dollars?" John gulped. "Where's he going to find that kind of money?"

Shrugging, Lian dropped her hand into her lap. "I thought about starting a crowdfunding page to generate some money from the community. But I'm open to any ideas."

"Send us a link to the web page." Jenn stood and grabbed the handle on the rolling suitcase. "We aren't exactly wealthy, but we'd like to contribute if it would help." She nodded to Rosa. "You guys have our email address." She hugged Rosa. "Thanks, dear. We'll send pictures of the grandbaby."

John gave everyone a round of hugs too.

When the front door closed, a blanket of calm settled in the dining room.

Rosa twirled the edge of her white apron. "When did Roman say he wanted to save the inn?"

Lian sighed. "Last night. We were walking back from dinner at the Beach House."

"Paula let him?"

Lian swallowed. How much should she tell Rosa about what she knew without violating Roman's trust and privacy? "He broke up with her. He's been staying at the carriage house."

"Gracias a dios," Rosa said, gripping the back of a chair. "How did you get him to come to his senses?"

"I didn't." A twinge of pain flickered in her body. He had been thinking of her all those years, waiting for her return, and now he wanted to save the inn and turn it into some place where they could both stay and start over. She sighed. "He did it on his own."

Rosa narrowed her gaze and wagged her finger. "That boy does nothing on his own. He always follows orders." She raised an arm over her head. "If Paula said to jump, he'd ask how high."

Was Roman that much of a people pleaser? Lian leaned against the back of the chair and took a sip of her lukewarm coffee. "He said he broke up with her because they wanted different things."

"Guess it doesn't matter how they broke up. Just matters that he's free." Rosa glanced around the room and huffed. "Are you sure he can keep the inn?"

"I don't know." Lian rubbed her forehead. A tightness squeezed her chest. She had already said too much. But she couldn't back down now, could she? "He's willing to do everything he can. This place is his home."

"Mine, too." Rosa nodded. "I mean, I don't live here, but I like working here, and I don't want to have to go someplace else." She made the sign of the cross and blew a kiss toward the ceiling. "May God save us."

Lian smiled. Whether or not she stayed, she could at least help Roman increase his odds of keeping this place. "Time to get working on that crowdfunding page." She swallowed the last gulp of coffee and stood. "The sooner we start collecting funds, the better our chances."

After a long day with a classroom full of students, Roman didn't look forward to an even longer afternoon paying the inn's expenses. But he had waited too long already. It was the last week of the month, and everything was due. He punched the access code into the lock on the front door and entered the lobby of the inn.

Rosa bustled out of the kitchen, wiping her hands in a dish towel. "We're saving the inn!"

"We are?" Roman scrunched his forehead. He had not told any of the staff his plans. "What are you talking about?"

Rosa pointed down the hallway. "Lian made a website for donations. We have five thousand dollars."

"We do?" Roman let the backpack slump off his shoulders. What website? What donations?

"Come and see." Rosa gestured with the dish towel.

After sliding the straps of the backpack over his shoulders, he followed Rosa down the hallway to the conference room. His vision wavered at the edges. Was he dreaming?

At the conference table, Lian sat in front of her laptop, typing, her eyes focused on the screen. She flicked her gaze upward and smiled. "Hi, Roman. Has Rosa told you what we're doing?"

"Kind of," he said, dropping his backpack at his feet and taking a seat next to her. The stack of coloring books and crayons towered on the other side of the table. His fingertips tingled with the memory of moving a crayon against the page. The prickling sensation moved up his wrist and into his arm until he could feel the memory of his elbow jostling against her arm, her breath so close it warmed his ear. He rubbed his hand against his forearm, blotting the memory of the touch. Had she colored last night?

In the doorway, Rosa waved the towel. "Show him the money."

After swiveling the screen, Lian pointed. "I built a web page on a crowdfunding site for the inn."

Roman angled the screen, scanning the pictures. Dozens of photographs showcased the history of the inn, from before his grandparents' purchase to today. A fuzzy feeling spread across his chest, and his tongue felt heavy in his mouth. "You did this today?"

Lian nodded.

"Where did you find these?" He pointed to the photographs of his grandparents sitting in wheelchairs in the courtyard by the koi pond. Even with their tufts of white hair, squinty eyes, and gummy smiles, they looked happy holding hands. He steeled his back, preparing for the reflexive jolt of tears, but only a dull ache throbbed behind his breastbone.

"The boxes in the attic," Rosa said. She picked up a folder on the table and withdrew a stack of photographs.

"I hope you don't mind," Lian said. "I scanned and sorted them into a collage for the website. And Rosa provided the email addresses of all the guests who've stayed here over the years, so we could contact them for donations."

Roman gaped. "But we've had thousands of people from all over the world visit."

Nodding, Lian smiled. "That's the beauty of mail merge programs."

Dumbfounded, Roman slumped against the chair and stared at the total of donations on the screen—over five thousand dollars.

Why hadn't he thought of this idea?

Lian touched his forearm. "I also contacted the local paper. Someone will be calling to interview you about the fundraising efforts for a front-page story."

"And my church will hold a bake sale," Rosa said.

Lian brightened. "I can make my cake cookies." The light dimmed from her face. "Depending on a few other things." Her voice trailed off.

"What other things?" Rosa asked.

"I have an opportunity to go overseas on a writing assignment," she said. "If I take it, I leave next week and I won't return until August."

Rosa pouted. "The bake sale will happen before you return."

"No worries," Lian said, nodding to the screen. "You might not need it the way donations are going."

"Every bit helps," Rosa said. "Isn't that right, Roman?"

He nodded, but his voice caught in the back of his throat. How could he ever repay Lian for her generosity and support? Especially if she was leaving. He glanced at her, but he could not read her expression. Was she still considering his offer to stay at the inn? His heart pinched. Or was she set on leaving?

A miasma of doubt clouded his head. Pulling the laptop close, he read what Lian had written.

Help Save Valentino Inn

When Davide and Marisa Valentino bought the inn thirty years ago, they dreamed of a place where people could go to be at home when they were traveling.

They lovingly remodeled the 1899 Queen Anne and transformed it into a Mediterranean masterpiece with a Spanish hacienda floorplan and touches from Tuscany. The nineteen rooms were decorated with museum quality antiques and featured first class hospitality from the homecooked meals by Marisa served on Sheffield silver and Victorian china to the daisies delivered daily to each room by grandson, Roman.

But during the past two years, both Davide and Marisa fell ill. To pay their medical expenses, they took out a reverse mortgage secured by the inn. With the downturn in travel from the pandemic, the inn's income plummeted. By the time they both passed away within weeks of each other, the inn was deeply in debt.

Working with minimal staff, the inn still manages to provide excellent food and hospitality, although Roman doesn't deliver daily daisies to the rooms anymore. He's too busy struggling to find the million dollars needed to repay the loan. And he has only two months left.

If you remember your time at the inn fondly and wish to donate, your contribution is greatly appreciated. If you can't help with money at this time, please share this request with friends and family who might be interested in preserving Valentino Inn's legacy of good food and hospitality in the heart of the Monterey peninsula.

He stared at the screen, his eyes unfocused, his heart overflowing. Leaning over, he hugged Lian, then stood to hug Rosa. "Thank you both. You don't know how much this means to me."

"Oh, yes, we do." Rosa kissed her fingers then pointed to the ceiling. "Nana and Pop know, too."

"And they approve," Roman said. He stooped to retrieve his backpack. A cloud of heaviness returned when he thought about the tasks at hand. No matter how much help he received, he still needed to take care of the ongoing business. "I'll be in the office paying bills, if either of you need me." Turning, he lumbered down the hall.

Alone in the tiny office, Roman shut the door and set his backpack on the cluttered desk. Rifling through stacks of paper, he located the bills. After logging online to check the balance in the operating account, he set up automatic payments for the water and utilities. Next, he sent funds to the bookkeeper for payroll. Finally, he brought up a copy of the property's appraisal. When it first arrived months ago, he had given it a cursory glance. Now he read it more carefully.

A knock on the door startled him. "Yes?" He glanced in the direction of the sound.

The door creaked open, and Lian peeked her smiling head inside. "Mind if I join you?"

"No problem." Roman cleared a stack of files from the chair beside him. "Have a seat."

"What are you doing?" Lian scooted close.

She smelled like lavender and honey. He breathed in more deeply, trying to capture and hold the memory of the scent. "I'm going over the appraisal."

Leaning closer, she stared at the screen. "You know, when I first arrived here, I went to the county thinking I could have this place registered as a historical site," she said. "But I was told the property was originally a Queen Anne and not a Spanish-Italian hybrid remodel."

"Historical status wouldn't save this place from foreclosure," Roman said.

"Is that why Paula paid for the permits for a new hotel-spa construction?" Lian asked.

Roman stopped reading. A cold sensation plunged through his body. "She what?"

"I thought you knew."

She looked at him with such wide eyes full of surprise that Roman didn't doubt her honesty. Shaking his head, he murmured. "Paula's a real estate agent. Why would she pull permits for construction?" He paused, mulling things over. "Unless she already has a client interested in the property." His jaw tensed.

"I don't know if she has a client," Lian said. "I was at the county offices talking to Tim. He told me Paula had come by a few weeks ago for a permit to build a spa hotel like the ones on Cannery Row."

A spa hotel. He cursed. A surge of anger powered through his body, and he curled his hands into fists. How could she betray him? A sharp pain stabbed the back of his head. "What else did Tim say?"

Lian gnawed on her lower lip and dipped her chin. "Well, he said you could remodel and restore this place. But supply chain issues and cost overruns might make it financially prohibitive." She lifted her chin and gazed at the appraisal on the screen. "Tim mentioned he worked as a carpenter on the remodel, so he was familiar with the property. When your grandparents bought the two parcels, they remodeled the main house but left the carriage house intact." She swallowed. "I'm sorry I thought you already knew this information. I assumed Paula had shared it with you."

Roman rubbed his forehead. "No, she didn't." What else had Paula kept from him? A sour taste filled his mouth. Had she willingly sabotaged his efforts to save the inn in the hopes of buying her dream home? A fresh surge of disbelief and anger fueled him. He scrolled to the top of the appraisal and began reading again.

Just as Lian said, the property was comprised of two individual parcels. Each parcel had a separate valuation in addition to a grand total, which was the figure the estate attorney had given him when discussing the property. The inn was estimated at a little over five million. The carriage house was worth a little over one million. Rubbing his jaw, he considered this information. Selling the carriage house, minus the fees and the commission, would give him enough to pay off the loan and keep the inn. He frowned, taking the scenario further. If he sold the carriage house, he would have to move. Could he envision staying in one of the rooms at the inn? He tapped his chin with a finger. A seed of hope sprouted.

Swiveling in his chair, Roman met Lian's gaze. He explained the appraisal and his proposition. "And with the funds from the campaign you and Rosa are running, we might have enough to refurbish this place to make it more presentable to the public."

"Like new mattresses," Lian suggested.

"Yes, and new chairs." He pointed to the squeaky wheels on the office chair.

She smiled. "And maybe you could hire more staff, so you won't have to work every weekend."

He laughed, and the pressure lifted from the back of his head. "I'm sure Rosa would appreciate two days off," he said.

Lian touched his arm. "Do you think Paula's willing to just list the carriage house?"

The concern in Lian's eyes mirrored the solid weight in his solar plexus. He didn't know how Paula would react to the request, but he didn't want to think about it tonight. "I'll call her tomorrow morning." He placed his hand over Lian's cool fingers. "Tonight, I want to make dinner for you to thank you for everything you've done for me and the inn."

She widened her smile, placing her other hand over his. "Only if you let me help."

"Deal," he said.

Chapter Twenty

Lian was washing the green peppers in the kitchen sink when her phone rang. After drying her hands on a dish towel, she grabbed the phone from her back pocket.

"Hello?"

"Lian, it's Jaz." Her voice was clipped and hurried. "I need to book that flight for Tuesday morning. Are you in?"

She glanced over her shoulder. Roman leaned into the fridge and the pantry, gathering ingredients and arranging them on the island. Every now and then, his gaze bobbed in her direction. When she caught the dark and curious look in his eyes, she tingled and turned away. "I don't know."

"What do you mean, you don't know? You've never balked at an assignment. What's changed?"

Everything. Lian swallowed, angling to the side. Roman hunched at the island, reading a torn and faded recipe book, his large hands bracing his arms on either side of the book. The dark veins cut rivers beneath his tanned skin, and the muscles in his forearms tensed. The dark hair fell over his bent head, shielding her from gazing into his large brown eyes. "I can't talk right now. I'll call you first thing on Monday."

"I've got meetings lined up all day. We're making a huge shift in design to attract a larger demographic. I'll text you my personal line. Let me know as soon as possible." Jaz sighed. "If you don't go, I'll need to find someone else."

Lian ended the call and shoved her phone deep into her pocket. Turning back to the sink, she finished rinsing the vegetables.

"Who was that?" Roman asked.

Lian shivered. The tone of his voice sounded proprietary, as if he had a right to an answer. If Matt had used that same inflection, she would have tensed, resisting a response. But she softened inside when she heard Roman's voice. He wasn't badgering her. He was inviting her to share. She grabbed a cutting board and placed a green pepper on its side. "My former editor."

"What did she want?"

Lian removed a chef's knife from the butcher block and started cutting. "She needs an answer about the trip."

Roman circled around the island. "Cut those a little smaller," he said. "Like this." He curled his hand over hers and guided it over the pepper, slicing the quartered pieces in half.

A quiver rippled up her arms, and her skin freckled in goose bumps. The warmth from his body and the heat of his breath kindled desire.

"Why did you put her off till Monday?" He removed his hand from her wrist and took a step back.

She gulped. "I haven't made up my mind." Wielding the knife, she tried to imitate his instructions. But some pieces still ended up larger than others.

He nodded. "Not bad."

She snickered. "Not good, either."

A muscle twitched in his jaw. "Are you considering staying here?"

The question rubbed against her like a striking match, sending a spark through her body. She set aside the knife and dried her hands. "Yes."

He pinned her with his hungry gaze. "I'd like you to stay."

Her breath caught in her chest. Should she stay? His pupils were so large they could swallow her. Her legs rooted to the floor, but her thoughts drifted away.

If she stayed, she would end up in a relationship with a much younger man who had his whole life ahead of him. He might want a family, and she could not give it to him. But if she left, even if the assignment didn't lead to a staff position, she could avoid the possibility of failing at love again.

"Please, stay." He touched her elbow.

She closed her eyes for a moment, letting the heat map her skin. When she opened them, she gazed into his longing eyes. "I can't have children."

He dropped his hand from her elbow and stepped back. "I'm not asking you to be the mother of my children. I'm asking you to stay and give us a chance."

Us. The word snagged in her mind. The way he had spoken it made her believe they were already a couple.

The doorbell chimed.

"We don't have any reservations," Roman said. "But sometimes we get walk-ins." He turned down the burner on the stove where the rice and chicken simmered. "I'll be right back."

Lian followed him into the lobby. What a different way of life. Never knowing when someone would show up. Always being ready to serve another. A constant flow of interruptions. She leaned against the doorjamb and crossed her arms over her chest. Could she adjust to this lifestyle?

Roman opened the front door.

A gusty breath of fog exhaled into the room, causing a brief chill. Lian shuddered, rubbing her arms with her hands.

"Welcome to Valentino Inn." Roman smiled at the couple entering the establishment. "Two for the night?"

"Yes, please." A feeble man plopped a burgundy suitcase next to the grandfather clock and wheezed. "I guess I'm a little out of shape. I wasn't expecting so many stairs."

"I'm sorry we need better signage. There's a handicap assessable entrance from the back," Roman said, waving to the south.

"Too late now." The man extended his hand. "I'm Steve. This is my wife, Loretta. We're on our way to San Diego to visit family. Do you mind us staying only one night?"

"No problem," Roman said, grabbing a tablet from the host stand. "I'm Roman Valentino, the owner, and this is my friend, Lian."

"Nice to meet you both," Lian said, extending her arm. The pleasure of experiencing someone new thrilled her the same way stepping off a plane in another country did.

Loretta was a short woman with a brassy halo of dark hair. She shook Lian's hand with a meaty grip. Huffing, she wiggled out of a cardigan sweater. "It's a lot warmer in here than outside. I didn't expect it to be so cold in California."

"Where are you from?" Roman asked.

"Oregon." Loretta folded the sweater into the crook of her arm. Narrowing her gaze, she took a step forward. "Are you going to charge us extra for only staying one night?"

"No, we won't," Roman said, smiling. "We're slow, and we understand not everyone has the luxury of staying two nights."

"Thank God," Loretta said, fanning her face with one hand. "We're trying to save money by driving instead of flying."

"Where in Oregon are you from?" Lian asked. Years ago, she had written a story about the top ten places to stay along the Oregon coast.

"Ashland," Loretta said.

Lian scrunched her forehead. "Isn't that where the annual Shakespeare festival is held?"

Steve accepted the tablet from Roman. "You a big fan of the bard?"

"I love *Romeo and Juliet*," Lian said, clasping her hands.

Steve filled in the information requested. "They're doing a modern version of that play now."

"Juliet lives in a camper." Loretta puckered her lips like she had bitten into a tart lemon. "She's basically homeless."

"And the music is hip-hop," Steve said, shaking his head.

Lian scrunched her forehead. "Sounds more like an updated *West Side Story*."

"Doesn't matter." Roman accepted the tablet and credit card from Steve. "Love is timeless. You can't judge it by its cover."

Lian chuckled. "That's a *book* by its cover."

Steve and Loretta joined in the laughter.

Roman handed Steve a skeleton key. "Your room is down the hall and across from the conference room," he said. "We serve breakfast from eight to ten. I can make a fresh pot of decaf before I leave at nine in the event you want some." He pointed toward the coffee bar.

"No, but something smells good." Loretta lifted her chin and sniffed. "And we haven't had dinner."

Roman glanced at Lian. "Would you mind sharing?"

Lian crooked her smile. What could she say? He was a host, and he was entitled to offer his guests whatever he wanted. "I don't mind."

"You're both welcome to a plate of paella. It's my grandmother's recipe."

"Oh, perfect," Steve said, grabbing the suitcase. "I haven't had paella in years."

Roman gestured to the dining room. "Dinner will be served in fifteen minutes."

"Just enough time to freshen up," Loretta said.

As soon as the guests left for their room, Roman turned to Lian and grabbed her hands. "Thanks for understanding."

"No problem." Lian followed him into the kitchen. "But you do understand if you live here, you'll be cooking for guests every night." She stood beside the island.

After washing his hands in the sink, Roman lifted the lid to the steaming pot and slid the chopped green bell peppers off the cutting board into the simmering mixture. "Then, we'll just have to add that to our amenities and rebrand ourselves as BB&D—bed, breakfast, and dinner." He stirred the paella and returned the lid to the pot. Next, he grabbed four plates of china. He set two on the island and the other two on silver serving trays.

Watching Roman work filled her with a sense of awe and admiration. He glided with such ease around the kitchen. Folding her arms over her chest, she tilted her head. Maybe gender roles didn't matter as much as she thought they did. Roman wasn't any less of a man because he liked to work with children and cook. She wasn't any less of a woman because she didn't know her way around a classroom full of children. Maybe if she learned to pick someone who understood and accepted who she was, then she wouldn't run into the same problems she encountered in her first marriage.

"Is there anything I can do to help?" Lian unfolded her arms and gestured to the platters.

"Just stand there and look beautiful." Roman grinned. "I'll be back for our quiet dinner together."

"Promise?" She raised her eyebrows.

He lifted one tray. "Unless you want to join the guests?"

"Do you?" She tilted her head and offered a teasing smile.

"Sometimes I'll take my breakfast in the dining room and mingle." He leaned against the swinging door. "But tonight, I want to be alone…with you."

He disappeared into the dining room, and Lian leaned against the island. The delicate smell of saffron and chicken and brothy vegetables lingered in the air. She traced a finger across the countertop. Could she spend a life at this inn, cooking and eating in this kitchen, sharing a life with this imaginative boy who had grown into such a resourceful man? She stopped her tracing and frowned. Or would she feel trapped like a bird with clipped wings?

"Bon appétit," Roman said. He placed a carafe of sparkling water on the table next to the breadbasket.

Steve and Loretta thanked him again.

Humming, Roman strode into the kitchen. "I hope you don't mind eating at the island," he said. "I know it's not the romantic evening I had planned but the inn needs business, and the couple looked a little haggard being on the road all day."

"I understand," Lian said, perching on a stool.

Roman ladled the paella onto a plate. "Is there anything you don't understand?"

Glancing up at the ceiling, Lian screwed her lips to the side. "I don't understand why you asked me that question."

Setting a plate before her, he shrugged. "Paula wasn't understanding. Sometimes Nana and Pop didn't understand. It's not like I come with an instruction manual."

Lian laughed. "Who does?"

"Exactly." Roman set his plate next to hers and hopped onto a stool. "Any sparkling water?"

"No, thanks. Tap is fine."

He poured her a glass from the kitchen sink. "Why don't you like sparkling water?"

She scrunched her face. "It's too fizzy." She waved toward the carafe. "You may drink it. I don't mind."

"I know you don't. Nothing bothers you. Everything is easy." Roman handed her the tap water and poured a glass of sparkling water for himself. The liquid danced against his tongue. "I'm starting to wonder why your marriage failed. Was Matt the opposite of you?"

Lian jabbed her fork into the chicken and rice. "He wasn't exactly difficult. But he had certain expectations that I didn't meet."

"Like what?" Roman draped a napkin over his lap and picked up his fork.

"Well, I couldn't have children." Lian slipped the fork into her mouth and chewed. She nodded, pointing to her plate with her fork. "This is good."

"You like it?" Roman smiled. He speared the chicken with the tines and lifted it into his mouth. "Not too bland?"

"No, it's perfect."

His mind circled back to her comment about children. A heavy weight tugged at the bottom of his stomach. He scooted closer, letting his knee nudge against hers.

She did not pull away but leaned her weight against him.

"I promise I won't have any expectations if you stay," he said.

Swallowing, she set aside the fork. "I don't want to disappoint you."

His stomach clenched, and he drew his knee away. "How could you possibly disappoint me?"

She bowed her head and folded her hands in her lap. "You absolutely adore children. I can't deprive you of the experience of being a father."

He braced his arms on either side of the plate. "I'm not getting involved with someone just to have children."

"But if you fall in love, you'll want to create a family, and I can't give you that." She raised her head, and tears glistened in her eyes.

The air squeezed out of his chest. That's why she wouldn't stay. She didn't want to disappoint him if the relationship became serious.

Nana was right. Believing in Lian coming back to marry him was no different than believing in Santa or the Easter Bunny. Just because he wanted it to be true didn't make it true.

He stood, gathered his half-eaten plate, and carried it to the sink. "When does your flight leave for Eastern Europe?"

"I'm not sure if I'm going," she said.

His stomach clawed with hunger. Ignoring its protests, he scraped the food into the compost. He rinsed the plate in warm water and placed it in the dishwasher. Without turning, he clutched the dish towel to his chest. "I think you should take the assignment." He steadied his voice. "Being away is the only place you'll ever feel at home."

Chapter Twenty-One

"…no one's home. Please leave a message." BEEP.

Lian paced across the flagstone patio of the courtyard. She jabbed her finger against the red button to end the call without leaving a message. Why wasn't her sister, Joanne, home after ten on a Friday night? She had small children. Oh, of course, Lian shook her head. Date night. The sitter wouldn't answer the phone. Why didn't she leave a message?

Glancing up at the night sky pricked with stars, she considered calling her other sister, Mindy, even though Mindy turned off the ringer at night after the kids went to bed, so she could sleep.

Lian grumbled. Sleep would be elusive now.

Tumbling into a wicker chair, she punched in Geeta's number. The phone rang a few times.

"Hey," Geeta said. "How's it going?"

"Not good." Lian stared at the tinkling fountain. The white fairy lights twinkled all around the perimeter of the inn, casting a magical glow. She breathed in and sighed, feeling the pulse of the inn strum within her like a big, beating heart. "I need your help."

"What happened?"

She swallowed, recalling the sudden shift in the conversation during dinner, and how Roman left to clean up before finishing his meal. "I've been spending a lot of time with the host here. And I think I'm falling in love with him." She scrunched her eyes closed and rubbed her forehead. Was love too strong a word for what she felt?

"Oh, my," Geeta said.

The tone of her cousin's voice echoed all around like a warning. "I know, I shouldn't feel anything for anyone. It's too soon after the divorce. But he's such a sweet guy, and he's in love with who I was when I first came here." A pain bloomed in her chest. "But I'm not that same person anymore."

"Oh, Lian," Geeta said. "Don't beat yourself up. We all change."

"Not everyone," Lian said. "Or everything." She opened her eyes and glanced around the ivy trailing up the stucco walls and the glowing lights inside the inn through the French doors. She smiled. "Some things stay exactly the same."

"So, how can I help?" Geeta asked.

Lian sighed, shifting her attention to the water plinking in the fountain beside her. "I've been offered an assignment. Eastern Europe. Three months. Roman suggested I go. But I think a part of me wants to stay." She bit her lower lip. "He pulled back after telling me to take the assignment. I think I hurt him. And I don't know how to make things right."

"Have you tried talking to him?"

She glanced over her shoulder at the dark passage leading to the carriage house. After cleaning up for the night, Roman said goodnight without offering a hug or a kiss. The memory chilled her. "What would I say?"

"Exactly what you've told me."

She snickered. "I don't think that would work. He wants me to make up my mind, and I can't."

"Do you need another reading?" Geeta asked.

"Would you mind?"

"I'll shuffle the cards. You tell me when to stop."

Breathing in deeply, Lian concentrated on the soft sounds of ruffling paper. "Stop."

"The five of swords reversed," Geeta said. "Well, that's interesting."

Lian listened to her pulse beat in her ears. "Is it bad?"

Geeta chuckled. "Not necessarily bad, but not necessarily good either." She paused. "Normally, the five of swords means something mentally is holding you back, but when it is reversed, it means you are letting go of something that no longer serves you."

Lian leaned back against the wicker chair and gazed up at the starry sky. "So, what exactly does that mean?"

Geeta lowered her voice. "What are your fears?"

Fears. Lian closed her eyes. She had too many of them. "I don't want to mess up another person's life."

"That's not your decision to make," Geeta said. "You only have control over your own life, and not anyone else's." She paused. "What do you want?"

Blinking, she wondered. "A home." She shifted her gaze to her sandaled feet. "Roman said I'd only ever feel at home while I'm on the road."

"Is that true?"

Lian sighed. Travel writing meant hiking, biking, kayaking, swimming, sailing, snorkeling, and swimming around the world. Caravanning through deserts and rain forests, through cities and farmland, from one continent to another. Restaurants and hotels. Planes and trains and automobiles. And strangers. Tons of people she would meet but never know. But, most importantly, a constant fence around her heart. "Traveling is what I know." She swept her gaze around the courtyard, taking in the peaceful tranquility of this lovely night. The walls of the inn sealed off the coastal fog and chill. Within its enclosure, she felt as safe, protected, and warm as she did in Roman's arms.

How could she walk away from that feeling?

"It's late," Geeta said. "You should try to get some sleep."

A bitter laugh escaped her mouth. "I'll just toss and turn and worry."

For a long moment, silence ached across the line.

Finally, Geeta said, "I've got to go. Try not to worry. You'll know you've fixed your problem once you sleep through the night."

"Thanks, Geeta. Goodnight." Lian ended the call. She stood and crossed the courtyard, returning to the warmth and silence of the inn. After climbing the stairs to her room, she got ready for bed and lay beneath the covers, staring at the ceiling. Focusing on the rise and fall of each breath, she tried to empty her mind. But the loop of constant chatter tumbled like a washing machine on spin cycle. Every mistake she had made, both from that night and all previous nights, dating back to her earliest memories, circled. Her chest ached, and her jaw tensed. How could she leave on Sunday without first making things right?

Where was she? Roman searched the conference room, the library, the lobby, and the dining room, but he couldn't find Lian. A dull ache throbbed in his chest. He needed to apologize for his behavior last night. That dismissive comment about how she should take the travel assignment because the road was her home had meant to push her away, not break his heart. And hers too. He winced, remembering the look of confusion on her face followed by the hooded eyes and the tremor in her chin.

"What are you doing here?" Rosa said, bustling into the dining room. "You have a meeting with the bruja."

Roman flinched. "Paula is not a witch."

"She's no saint," Rosa said, gathering the dishes from breakfast.

The scent of poached eggs and sugary cinnamon rolls lingered in the thick air. Gritting his teeth, Roman silently cursed. Why hadn't he closed the office door when he was talking to Paula this morning? That way Rosa wouldn't know about his meeting with her at eleven to discuss business. Roman raked his fingers through his hair. "I'm waiting for Lian. I need to talk to her before I leave."

"She's probably still sleeping. That girl works too much." Rosa shook her head, hugging the silver platter full of china. "You know last night before I went to bed, I checked the website." She grinned. "Guess how much we've raised?"

"How much?" Roman didn't know how high to guess.

Rosa smiled. "Twenty thousand dollars."

"We have?" Roman crinkled his forehead. Unbelievable.

Nodding, Rosa shifted the weight of the tray to one hip. "I wonder how much more we'll raise over the weekend."

The grandfather clock chimed eleven.

"You're late," Rosa said, turning to leave. "You'd better go unless you want her to turn you into a toad."

"I'm going." He glanced around the room one last time before threading his arms through the backpack. An empty feeling numbed his body. He'd have to talk to Lian later.

He opened the front door and bounded down the stairs in the warm sunlight. Across the street, the waves rocked along the craggy shoreline. Harbor seals barked, and gulls swooped. People crowded the trail. He stuck to the sidewalk along Ocean View Boulevard, his gaze fixed toward the café in the near distance.

Time to face the witch.

Chapter Twenty-Two

Paula sat at her favorite table against the full-length windows overlooking Lovers Point Beach with her briefcase opened and her laptop ready to discuss whatever business Roman wanted. She had already finished her mocha. The black coffee with cream and no sugar, which she bought for Roman, was probably lukewarm at best. She glanced out the window at the bright sky and the sidewalk full of tourists and families out and about for the weekend, but she didn't see his tall, lanky figure in the crowd. She tapped her freshly manicured nails against the white tabletop and pursed her lips. Where was he? She had another appointment in an hour—a lunch date with a contractor who had been eyeing her for years. But she would cancel if Roman wanted to get back together. She squinted at the clock on her computer. Five after eleven. She would grant him ten more minutes before she would pack up and leave.

Four minutes later, Roman nudged the glass door open with one shoulder and marched across the hardwood floors of the modern café. She snickered. He looked like a haggard college student with his long sleeve shirt untucked around torn jeans and dirty sneakers. As he approached, he rubbed a hand along the day-old scruff dusting his cheeks and chin. His dark hair flopped over his forehead, and a worried expression troubled his brown eyes.

"Hey, sorry I'm late." He slouched into the chair across from her and set his backpack on the seat next to him.

"You're always late," she said. A bristle of annoyance shimmied up her spine. No *Hello, how are you?* Or *I miss you. Good to see you again.* She expected him to say something soft and sensible to bridge the gap between coupledom and singledom. His greeting of *Hey, sorry I'm late* sounded like an excuse. "I have an appointment at noon on the other side of town." She fudged the distance, hoping to make him feel guilty.

"I'll make this brief." He unzipped the main pocket of the backpack and removed a set of papers. Turning to a specific page, he pointed to a line. "The appraiser mentioned the property is composed of two separate parcels. He even gave them their own valuations." He tapped the number in the second column.

"Where are you going with this exercise?" She narrowed her gaze. A lot of properties were comprised of more than one parcel given the history of this place. Everyone knew Pacific Grove was established as a religious retreat by David Jacks in the 1800's. The hundred acres were subdivided into thirty-by-sixty-foot lots for camping around Lovers of Jesus Point, which had been shortened over the years to Lovers Point.

"So," Roman said, smiling.

"So?" Paula tensed. His eyes were bright. His voice was eager. He was happy. Not about seeing her again, but about his grandparents' property. The same property that had given him nothing but troubles. Why had he come here to talk about the appraisal? A niggle of fear wiggled up the backs of her legs. What was she missing?

Roman tapped the paper again. "I want to modify the listing agreement. I want to sell only the carriage house for 1.2 million dollars."

Roman braced for attack. Surely, Paula would launch into a detailed explanation of a dozen or so reasons why he had to sell both parcels.

But Paula slumped in the chair across from him. No sound emerged from her slackened mouth and parted lips. She wasn't expecting this proposal.

He tapped his fingers against the table. Did she think he had arranged this little meeting as a cover up to get back together, and not talk about business? A frown creased his face. He had no intention of getting back together. He didn't even miss her. He only cared about selling a portion of the property. In particular, the carriage house.

After a couple of staggering moments, Paula blinked several times. "If you sell the carriage house, where will you go?"

"The inn. There's plenty of rooms." Roman pointed to his chest. "It's just me. I don't need much." Except Lian. A dull ache throbbed beneath his breastbone.

"I see." Leaning across the table, Paula flipped to the next page and pointed to the diagram. "There's only one problem. The carriage house and the inn share the courtyard." She traced the outline with the tip of her finger.

"How do you propose to divide up that space with a new owner?"

"I'm not worried," Roman said. If the new owner wanted the courtyard, the new owner could pay extra.

"You should be." Paula tapped her finger on the image. "No family wants to share a backyard with a bed and breakfast."

"A family?" A cold, hard stone plunged to the bottom of his stomach. He moved aside the cup of coffee and folded his arms on the sticky table. "The permits you pulled aren't for a family." His voice was a blade of steel. "They're for a spa hotel."

Widening her eyes, Paula flinched. "Who told you?"

Icy rays spread throughout his body, pricking his nerves. Roman scoffed. "Is that all you care about—who told me?" He straightened his spine and wagged a finger at her. "*You* should have told me." A muscle twitched in his jaw. "You kept this information a secret because you knew I had to sell both parcels in order for us to buy your dream home." His voice chilled. "You care more about yourself than you care about me."

"The same sentiment can be said about you." Grimacing, Paula rifled through her briefcase. "You care more about that inn than you've ever cared about me." She tugged two sheets of paper from a folder and ripped them into tiny pieces, tossing the confetti-like remnants on the table. "Go sell the carriage house—without me." She stood, holding her laptop case in one hand and the briefcase in the other. "Goodbye, Roman. I hope we never see each other again." Swiveling, she stalked out of the café in her white blouse, black skirt, and high heels—a paradigm of cold-hearted business.

Taking a deep breath, Roman raked a hand through his hair. He hadn't wanted to upset her. He only wanted the truth. But her reaction only confirmed what he already knew. He had made the right choice.

Sighing, he stared out the window at the gray skies and the crowds of tourists and families scattered on the sidewalk. The tension in his jaw eased, and the chill left his body.

What had he ever seen in her? He plucked the scattered pieces of the torn listing agreement off the table. The wadded ball of paper pulsed in his fist. Maybe he never loved her, only the image she projected. She was the adult he thought others expected him to be—practical and business-minded. But he was fine being who he was— imaginative and playful—a competent, capable adult who could make it on his own.

Standing, he strode across the café and shoved the balled-up paper into the trash. Returning to the table, he removed a five-dollar bill from his wallet and tucked it beneath the empty mug that stank of burnt coffee and chocolate. He flipped the appraisal to the front page and tucked it into his backpack. After zipping up the pocket, he threaded his arms through the holes and let the weight settle against his back. Before he left, he scanned the business cards on the corkboard by the entrance, searching for a new real estate agent, someone he could hopefully trust.

Chapter Twenty-Three

Lian yawned and stretched. Light leaked into the room from the edges of the curtains. She rubbed her eyes and flipped over her phone. The green light flickered with a message. Her breath hitched. Had Roman sent a text? She struggled into a sitting position and tapped the screen. Twelve o'clock. She gasped. Was it really noon? She remembered falling asleep just as the birds twittered in the distance and a gray light softened the shadows. But she didn't expect to sleep through breakfast. Again. She swiped her finger across the screen and read the message.

—*How are you doing today?*—

Her shoulders slumped against the pillow. The message was from Geeta. Not Roman. Quickly, she typed a response.

—*Groggy. Overslept.*—

She clutched the phone to her chest. A few seconds later, her phone pinged with a response.

—*Enjoy your last day in paradise.*—

The message was a double-edged sword. How could she enjoy today when she was still worried about last night? Grumbling, she slipped out of bed and freshened up before bounding down the stairs. The dining room doors were closed and locked, as they were normally during the day. Turning, she pumped some coffee into a paper cup and stirred in some creamer. The bitter liquid stung her tongue. She was about to head back up to her room when she heard someone call her name.

"Lian," Rosa said, hustling over. "There you are. Guess how much we've raised?"

"How much?" Lian shrugged. How much could they have raised overnight?

"Thirty thousand dollars." Rosa danced around in a circle, waving her hands overhead.

Lian tightened her clamped fingers around the paper cup. "That's a lot." With a lot more to go.

"Come, you haven't had breakfast." Rosa ushered Lian into the kitchen. "I saved some food for you."

Comforting memories from last night floated through Lian's mind before the conversation twisted toward the possibility of her leaving with no definite date of return. A sour taste filled her mouth. Why had she ruined the evening by picking up Jaz's phone call?

After setting her cup of coffee on the island, Lian plunked down on a stool and propped her head in her hands.

"You don't look too good," Rosa said. "You have a headache or something?"

Groaning, Lian rubbed her face. "I'm just confused."

"About what?" Rosa opened the refrigerator and set a platter of food in the microwave.

Dropping her hands to her lap, Lian bit her lower lip. Should she confide in Rosa? "I think I upset Roman last night."

"Ah, that's why he wanted to talk to you." Rosa grabbed a mug from a cabinet and poured fresh coffee into it. She slid it across the island and set a carton of half-and-half next to it.

"Thanks." Lian lifted her paper cup. "I already have some."

Rosa snatched the paper cup from her hand and nodded toward the mug. "That's better." She dumped the coffee into the sink and tossed the paper cup into the recycling bin. "So, tell me what you did to upset him."

Lian accepted the spoon Rosa offered and stirred the cream into the coffee. "We've been spending a lot of time together." She took a sip of the hot coffee and let the warmth slide down to loosen the knot in her stomach. "We talked about the possibility of building a relationship, but he wants me to be here and I'm not sure if I want to stay." She paused, catching the look of surprise in Rosa's eyes. "When my old employer called last night to discuss an opportunity for me to work overseas for three months, he suggested I leave." She heaved a sigh. "He stopped eating and started putting things away. When I mentioned it again, he refused to talk." She blinked, cupping the warm mug in both hands. "I didn't sleep well knowing things weren't right between us." She glanced up into Rosa's steady gaze. "You know him better than I do. How can I make things better?"

"Aye, dios mio." Rosa made the sign of the cross and pressed her palms together. "I pray every night for him to find a good woman. Not someone selfish like Paula. And look who God sent—you!"

"I don't think I'm a good woman," Lian said.

"Why not?" The buzzer dinged on the microwave, and Rosa removed the heated plate and set it before Lian. "I think you are. And Roman does, too. You care about things, and you like to help people."

Rosa had a point. Lian wasn't a bad woman. She was a broken one. "I can't have children," Lian explained. "And Roman would make such a good father."

"You're thinking too far ahead." Rosa set a napkin rolled with silverware next to the plate. "If you stay, you get to know each other better. Then you decide. If you go, you stay in touch and visit." With a dish towel, she wiped a spot on the island. "I don't see why you need to pick one or the other. Both will work."

Lian jabbed her fork into a piece of sausage and chewed. The juicy spices coated her tongue. What Rosa said made sense. Why hadn't she thought of that solution?

Roman was standing at the crosswalk waiting for a break in the weekend traffic when his phone rang. He dug the phone out of his pocket and swiped his finger across the screen. "Hello?"

"May I speak with Roman Valentino?"

"Speaking."

"Mr. Valentino, this is Greg Waters with the *Gazette*. I wanted to know if I could come by today and interview you about the crowdfunding efforts to save your inn."

A soft spot of tenderness bloomed in his chest. The reporter Lian promised had called. How could he have been so callous and immature last night when she wanted to discuss her options? His throat closed. Why had he pushed her away? She only wanted what was best—for him, for herself, for each other. He gritted his teeth. He needed to find time to talk to her tonight when he returned to the inn.

"I'm booked today." The traffic finally cleared, and Roman stepped off the Point Pinos Coastal Trail and crossed the street. "Can you come by tomorrow?" The spring skies were clear and blue, the air tepid and calm. A perfect day to show a reporter around the inn, if he had time, but he didn't. He needed to find a new real estate agent this afternoon.

"We want to run the story tomorrow as a full-page spread, if that's all right with you."

Sunday, full page spread. Roman gulped. That would get a lot more attention than the weekday news. And the inn needed publicity. He gripped the phone tighter. "I'm on my way to an appointment, but I can talk right now."

"Good," Greg said.

While Roman answered a series of questions, he passed the inn and turned the corner toward the entrance of the carriage house. Unlocking his four-door sedan, he slid inside and started the engine. The phone switched to the hands-free device, broadcasting Greg's voice on the stereo speakers. Roman tugged the seatbelt across his lap and shifted into Reverse, heading downtown to interview the four real estate agents he found from the business cards at the café. As he drove, he told Greg about the inn's history, its current situation, and the crowdfunding campaign.

"Thank you, Mr. Valentino," Greg said. "Do you have time for me to stop by and take a few pictures of the inn?"

"No, but you can call Rosa. She should be able to show you around." Roman gave Greg the number. "Anything else?"

"No, I think I have enough," Greg said. "Thank you for your time."

After ending the call, Roman pulled into the parking lot of the first real estate office on Lighthouse Avenue. He had purposefully avoided calling anyone from Paula's office, which was located two doors down. Taking a deep breath of the clean air, he slung his backpack over one shoulder. He glanced up at the sky and thought of Nana and Pop. *Please, let me find the right person to sell your home.*

Chapter Twenty-Four

The bell chimed, and Lian glanced up from a book she was reading in the library. She had messaged Roman earlier, asking when they could talk, and he had responded by saying as soon as he found a real estate agent to list the carriage house. Hoping the process wouldn't take too long, she had settled on the chaise beside an antique lamp to read an old copy of *The Great Gatsby*, which she hadn't read since high school. The paper crinkled when she turned the pages, a faint musty scent wafting in the air.

Rosa hustled to the door, her footsteps slapping on the hardwood floor. She wrung her apron in her hands. "Coming!"

Dipping her head, Lian tried to ignore the clamor of the door opening and the low guttural voice of a man. But when she overheard Rosa talking to Greg Waters from the *Gazette*, Lian set aside the book and uncurled from the comfortable chaise.

Greg looked like a seasoned photojournalist with his camera dangling from his neck and a notebook and pen in his hand. His wavy hair was peppered with white, and his hazel eyes crinkled at the corners when he smiled.

"Mr. Waters," Lian said, extending her arm. "I'm Lian Shu who contacted you about the story."

"Yes, Ms. Shu, thank you for the lead." Greg shook her hand. "I already spoke with Roman. I'm just here to take some pictures for tomorrow's paper."

Rosa gestured to the staircase. "I can give you a tour."

"That would be wonderful," Greg said, following Rosa.

"Wait." Lian raised her hand. "I'm a fellow writer and a friend of Roman. Is it possible to let me know what you plan to write for the article?" She didn't want the publicity to shine a poor light on the inn.

Greg cleared his throat. "Well…you know it's not customary to run a story by a source. Maybe the direct quotes."

"I'm just concerned," Lian said, clasping her hands to her chest. "I have a particular attachment to this place, and I want you to showcase it in the right light." She waved him into the library and pointed to the framed article on the wall. "I wrote about this place for *Getaway* magazine when it opened thirty years ago, and I thought that maybe if the *Gazette* could write a follow-up piece that ties the past together with the present, then Roman might have a better chance of drumming up business."

Greg slouched before the article, squinting at the print. "Is that you and Roman in the picture?" He arched an eyebrow and tapped the glass.

"Yes," Lian said, feeling her face tingle. "He used to bring fresh daisies to the rooms every morning."

"And now?"

"Well...a lot has changed." Lian swept her gaze around the library, suddenly viewing everything through Greg's eyes. From the poor lighting to the overstuffed bookshelves to the faded rugs and the dusty baby grand piano, the room didn't exude nineteenth-century glamor. The room looked as old and shabby as an establishment that had fallen into disrepair.

Greg bowed his head, reading the article. When he finished, he humphed. "Why aren't you writing this story?"

A wave of shame washed over Lian's face. "I'm currently unemployed. With no one traveling the past two years, *Getaway* magazine laid off most of the staff, including me."

"I see." Greg straightened his spine. "I'm here to report on the crowdfunding campaign. I don't have time to write a feature article. But if you'd like, you could write up a piece, and I can present it to my editor for tomorrow."

Lian widened her eyes, thinking of the original article she had pitched to Jaz. Her fingers itched to start typing. "How many words?"

"Between 1,000 and 2,000," he said. "The editor will probably cut it. But it's better to have too much than not enough."

"Okay, I'll do it." She buoyed with lightness. "What's the deadline?"

From the lobby, the grandfather clock struck two.

Greg lifted his eyebrows. "Can you have it to me in three hours?" He removed a business card from the inside pocket of his tweed jacket. "Send it to my email, and I'll forward it to my editor with a note explaining our conversation."

"Great. Thank you." Lian beamed, clutching the card to her chest. "I'll get started right away."

Nodding, Greg turned to Rosa. "I'm ready for that tour whenever you are."

"Right this way." Rosa waved toward the lobby.

Greg stepped out of the library.

Before Rosa followed, she gave a thumbs up to Lian. "Good job."

Lian quietly squealed, hugging the card. Good job, indeed.

After three interviews over three hours, Roman doubted he would find a suitable real estate agent to list the carriage house. The first agent had wanted to turn the property into a vacation rental. If Roman thought that idea was good, he would have leased out the rooms himself. The second agent suggested selling the property as a tear-down. "The only worth is in the land," the agent said, without having a site visit. "And the land is only worth five hundred thousand." The third agent, who he saw after a break for lunch at an Italian deli, predicted no one would want half a property. "You can't do anything with it."

Now Roman slouched in a scratchy chair in a tiny fluorescent-lit lobby waiting for the fourth and final real estate agent to see him. The flickering lights bothered his eyes. The dismal surroundings—a chipped coffee table housing decades old magazines and a water cooler that burped whenever anyone poured a glass—soured his already despondent mood. Maybe he should just leave.

After waiting fifteen minutes, Roman stood, slung his backpack over one shoulder, and strode toward the door.

"Are you Roman Valentino?" a gruff voice asked.

With one hand on the sticky doorknob, Roman glanced over his shoulder. An old man in a crumpled suit hunched over a walking stick. The guy looked like he should be visiting a doctor's office, not running a real estate business. Roman gulped. "Yes."

"I'm Albert Luchessi," the old man said, extending a hand.

Roman accepted the handshake. The old man squeezed, nearly crushing Roman's fingers. When the handshake ended, Roman shook his numb fingers. The old man was much stronger than he looked.

"I'm sorry to keep you waiting," Albert said. "But my secretary doesn't work weekends. Follow me." As he turned around in the hallway, he wobbled against the walking stick. "My office is the first door on the right."

The small room stank of coffee and cigarettes.

Roman sank into the chair across from a large desk littered with paper.

"Don't worry. I know where everything is," Albert said, lowering into his seat. "So, I hear you need to sell a property."

With one swift movement, Roman unzipped the backpack and handed Albert the appraisal. "Just the carriage house. It's the second property listed on page two."

Albert accepted the papers with trembling hands. After sliding a pair of reading glasses up the bridge of his nose, he flipped the page and peered at the diagram. "Yes, I see. The carriage house of Valentino Inn." He lowered the page and smiled, exposing crooked teeth. "My wife and I sent our relatives to the inn when we celebrated our anniversary five years ago." He nodded toward his computer, an ancient desktop with a monitor. "I saw your email about the fundraising project. Don't you want to wait to see if you raise enough so you don't have to sell?"

Roman squirmed. "The bank will take back both parcels if I don't repay the reverse mortgage in two months."

"I see," Albert said.

"I want to list the carriage house for 1.2 million dollars." Roman scooted to the edge of the seat. "I'm interested in selling the place to someone who doesn't mind sharing the backyard, which currently operates as a courtyard for the inn." He inhaled sharply and sat back. "Unless a developer wants the whole thing for an additional cost."

Albert finished reading the appraisal. He set the document on top of a leaning stack of papers and focused on the computer. For several seconds, he tapped on the keyboard and nodded. "I have a buyer who's been looking for something he can live in half the year and rent out for the other. Let me call him if you don't mind."

"Right now?" Roman leaned forward and clasped his hands between his knees. He didn't expect anyone to start calling around for buyers without signing some paperwork first.

"Yes, I'm sure he's around." Albert lifted the handset of a touch-tone phone on his desk and punched in the numbers. He rocked back and forth on the office chair. The bearings whined and creaked beneath the moving weight. "Charlie." He smiled. "Long time no chat, right? Hey, listen. I have an opportunity you might be interested in. The guy who owns Valentino Inn needs to sell a portion of the property." Nodding, he licked his lips. "Yeah, on Ocean View Boulevard. Not the main property. The one in the back. That's right. The carriage house. Four bedrooms, three bathrooms, almost 2,000 square feet and half a courtyard." He chuckled. "That's right. Shared with the inn. Hold on a second. He's here. Let me put you on speaker." Albert set the handset down on another stack of papers and punched a button on the keypad. "Can you hear me?"

"Yes, sir, loud and clear," Charlie said.

"Roman, this is Charlie. Charlie, this is Roman."

"Hi, Charlie," Roman said, leaning toward the speaker.

"Good to meet you, Roman," Charlie said. "I don't know how much Albert told you, but I have been waiting for the perfect place. Close to the beach, low maintenance yard, easy to rent in the months I'm not there. Your place sounds perfect. When can I see it?"

"Umm..." Roman widened his eyes. "As soon as it's listed."

"Listed? I want to write an offer before everyone crowds me out again. How much do you want for this place?"

"One point two million," Roman said.

A moment of silence filled the closet-sized office.

"Okay, Albert," Charlie said. "Write it up. I'll come by the property once the offer is accepted. Is that okay, Roman?"

Roman shook his head. "I don't understand." He had spent the past three hours listening to agents rattle on and on about their services. How could someone just pick up a phone and call a buyer to negotiate a sale without a listing agreement?

Albert swiveled in his chair. "What don't you understand?"

"This." Roman waved back and forth across the table and pointed to the phone. "You're honestly going to write an offer sight unseen on a home that isn't listed?"

Albert chuckled. "This is old school real estate." He sat upright, and the chair squeaked. "Unless you want all that fancy internet marketing and strangers trampling through your home during an open house."

Shaking his head, Roman pursed his lips. "I just want to sell the place."

"Then let me write the offer with Charlie," Albert said. "Then we can talk about the listing."

This backward process stunned Roman into silence. A fuzzy understanding wavered at the edges of his mind. Paula had approached her sellers to buy their home before it hit the open market, and now Albert had just offered Roman's property to a client before it was listed. That's how business was done. Roman leaned back against the hard wooden chair and crossed an ankle over his knee. Albert considered his current client's needs before roping a new client into a listing agreement. A lightness spread across Roman's chest. That's exactly who he wanted to do business with, someone who thought of others before themselves. "Okay." He nodded to Albert. "Let's do it."

Chapter Twenty-Five

With her back propped up with pillows, Lian sat on the lace bedspread in her room overlooking the bay and reread the unfinished draft of the article she had written for the *Gazette*. Every now and then, she leaned over and tapped the keyboard to correct a word or phrase.

A week ago, I returned to the first location I visited when I started my career as a travel writer almost thirty years ago. I wanted to recapture a sense of hope and romance after a painful divorce left my self-esteem shattered.

But when I arrived, the inn had changed.

The once pristine driveway sheltered by lattice had been overgrown with mold and moss. The bright pink exterior had faded to a dirty blush. The arched windows were smudged. Even the potted plants along the crumbling stone staircase had wilted. The beautiful mansion by the bay I remembered had fallen into disrepair. My dreams of recapturing the enthusiasm of my youth through this place crumpled.

When I stepped into the shabby lobby with its faded rugs and peeling floral wallpaper, I smelled the dank and musty odors of a home that had not aged well. Time had added a dull patina to everything, from the baby grand piano in the library to the rickety chairs in the dining room to the wild ivy growing on the walls in the courtyard.

Even the little boy who had delivered fresh daisies to my room every morning had grown up.

She paused, her fingers hovering over the keyboard. But that little boy had aged very well. A fresh flush rushed through her body, warming her fingertips. He was a young man now, and more handsome than anyone she had ever met. Why did she let this thought distract her?

When I discovered upon my arrival the inn was closing the following week and being sold to pay off the debt accumulated by the original owners when they had fallen ill and died, I felt a rush of nostalgia and a pang of regret. Just like I could not hold onto the ideal dreams I had for a wonderful marriage, I could not hold onto the illusions I had of this Mediterranean paradise by the bay.

Disheartened, I questioned everything about my life—from the career I had lost during the pandemic to the children I could not have and the marriage that had failed to the future that loomed dark and foggy in the distance. The despair left me restless.

Except the moments she spent with Roman. She dropped her hands into her lap, remembering the tenderness of his strong arms circling her body and the tenderness of his kiss. Oh, how she found more comfort in his touch than she had with the stuffed otter she purchased at the gift store or the quiet moments walking alone on the beach. Sighing, she missed the peacefulness and contentment she experienced sitting side-by-side coloring in the conference room. No matter what was going on around her, she always felt safe and secure whenever he was nearby.

Pausing, she glanced out the window. The sky burned a brilliant blue, and the ocean waves lapping along the shore sang a lullaby. Whenever she traveled, she often slept better than she had at home. But here, the process was reversed. Why could she not find rest?

Without waiting for an answer, she dipped her head and continued reading.

Over the next few days, I wandered around Pacific Grove and Monterey, doing everything a tourist would— visiting the aquarium, dining on Cannery Row, driving the scenic route through Pebble Beach, spending a day in Carmel, and hiking the trails at Point Lobos.

I was searching for my lost self, not realizing I would not find her. She was gone.

She sucked in a breath. How did the essay end? She didn't know. She had never found a new version of herself.

Tapping her chin with a finger, she stared at the laptop screen. Four-thirty. Only thirty minutes until she must submit her story. Her heartbeat ratcheted in her chest. For the first time in her career, would she miss a deadline?

Three knocks on the door startled her. She saved her work and scooted off the mattress. Her legs tingled and her back ached. "Who is it?"

"Roman."

The sound of his voice propelled her to the door. She stumbled on the pins-and-needles prickling the soles of her feet.

"May I come in?" he asked.

He stood beneath the threshold dressed in a button-up shirt with sleeves cuffed around his forearms, a pair of faded jeans, and dirty sneakers. Physically, he looked the same, but a quiet confidence radiated from his smile.

"Sure." She stepped aside and swung the door fully open.

Striding into the room, he gazed at the laptop. "Are you checking on the campaign?"

A protectiveness over her unfinished writing swelled, and she rushed over to the laptop to shut the lid. "No, I'm writing a personal essay for the *Gazette*." Her whole body tingled. "I don't know if they'll print it. I promised Greg a feature article, but I keep turning the focus back on how this place makes me feel." She shifted her stance, rocking back and forth between her feet. An ache all out of proportion gripped her insides. Everything she thought to be lasting about this place had either disappeared or transformed, including the memory of the young woman she had been, and the boy Roman once was.

She glanced up at him. An uneasy feeling rippled across her scalp. Something about him had changed. What was it? Squinting, she studied him closer. But she couldn't name the difference. Shifting her focus, she waved a hand at the laptop. "I have thirty minutes before I submit the essay, and I can't find an ending to the story."

"Because your story doesn't end," he said, taking her hands in his.

The meaningful look in his eyes made her shiver. He squeezed her hands three times. Once for *I am here*. Twice for *I care*. Three times for *I love you*.

Heat invaded her body, and she glanced away. "I want to believe you." She squeezed his hands twice, but she could not pull away. Her feet had sprouted roots through the carpet, anchoring her.

"Then believe me." He released one hand and tilted her chin until he could look into her eyes.

The scorching gaze seared through her, and she smoldered with an unexplainable desire to melt against him until the lines between their bodies blurred into one indistinguishable mass.

She blinked. But she could not unsee what she had seen. That woman she was had died, and a new one had been born—into love for this man. How could she leave and go back to her apartment when she had finally, finally found her home in him? She squeezed his hands a third time. "I do."

He bowed his head and kissed her.

She parted her lips and welcomed his tongue into her mouth, tasting the sweetness of his love.

She's staying. Roman darted his tongue in and out of Lian's mouth, his hands gently cupping her back. He drifted in the undertow of the kiss, dizzy with visions of the future. Summer remodeling at the inn, fall festivities in the courtyard, winter evenings decorating the Christmas tree in the lobby. Finally, he broke away from her lips. "Wow." He panted. "What just happened?"

Lian giggled, her face flushed pink. "I just said yes, I'll stay at the inn." She leaned forward on her tiptoes and pecked his nose. "I'll be your girl."

"My woman," he corrected, tipping his head against hers. "I thought I had good news when I arrived, but this is the best news by far."

"You have good news?" She glanced up at him with wide eyes.

A broad smile stretched across his face. The muscles in his cheeks tensed with joy. "I think I sold the inn."

"Already?" She gaped. "That was fast."

"I know." He chuckled and gripped her waist. "A real estate agent had a buyer looking for a place like the carriage house. He wrote an offer sight unseen, and I accepted it on the condition that he view and approve the property within ten days."

"That's amazing." She twirled her fingers into his hair. "We should celebrate."

He rubbed his nose against her neck. "What would you like to do?"

"Hmm…I'm open to ideas."

He pressed tiny kisses along her jawline.

She stiffened and pulled back. "My deadline!"

Dropping his arms from her back, he released her. Dread threatened to dampen his mood before he remembered she was writing a story for the benefit of the inn. He waved toward the laptop. "Go finish your story. I'll meet you downstairs for appetizers, then we'll go to the Beach House to celebrate."

Smiling, she wrapped her arms around his neck and tugged him close for one last kiss.

Her lips tasted slick and smooth and sweet with happiness. Sighing, he squeezed her close before letting her go.

When he stood beneath the threshold with his hand on the doorknob, he glanced at her one last time. Something about her had changed. To a stranger, she might look the same—long black hair swinging down her back and her slender body clad in a T-shirt and jeans. But to him, she radiated a sense of peace. That restless energy that kept her up each night was finally gone.

Chapter Twenty-Six

Lian swept her hair away from her sweaty face and twirled it into a ponytail, fastening it with an elastic tie from the dresser. She tugged the laptop toward her and tapped her fingers against the edge of the keyboard. She had fifteen minutes to write an ending to her story for the *Gazette*.

Think, think, think.

Deep breath, focus.

In thirty years, she had never missed a deadline. She would not miss one now.

She reread what she had written so far about a lost woman seeking to recover her identity through revisiting her past. The thought that someone, and not something, could save her never entered her mind. Envisioning Roman, she typed.

That boy who had grown up at the inn was gone too.

He was a young man now. An elementary school teacher who shepherded his students with loving guidance. A man who valued the lessons his grandparents had taught him—about a generous hospitality that gifted their guests with a sense of belonging.

That sense of belonging inspired me to return to the inn. I believed I could rescue my future by revisiting the past. But upon my arrival, I learned the inn would close after one week. The shock spiraled me into restlessness. How could everything I took to be lasting and real disappear?

Over the week, in the safety of this home away from home, I confronted the truth. I traveled to avoid the mess of my life, from my inability to have children to my failed marriage. With sadness and disillusionment, I grieved the losses. Most importantly, through the help of the young man who owned the inn, I learned to welcome the new woman I was becoming, a woman who had been given one more chance to create a life she did not need to escape.

My decision to launch a fundraising campaign to save the inn originated out of nostalgia, but my decision to stay and help revitalize the inn comes from a deep love and respect for Roman Valentino and the memory of his beloved grandparents who believed everyone deserves a place to belong.

Lian ran a spelling and grammar check before attaching the document to an email, explaining her decision to write an essay instead of a feature article. As soon as she pressed Send, she glanced at the clock on the screen. With a laugh, she punched the air. She had made her deadline with one minute to spare.

Roman thought the dinner at the Beach House had been fabulous—a seafood medley for him, and a shrimp gumbo for Lian—and dessert had been delicious—a shared cup of chocolate mousse. The low chatter of couples and families surrounded them along with the scent of citronella from the candle flickering in frosted glass. Heat from tall lanterns radiated across the deck, but nothing compared to the warmth of Lian's hand in his.

Shadows flickered, and he squeezed her hand. "I'm sorry about my behavior last night." He bowed his head, releasing the burden. "I'm ashamed of my immaturity. I need to learn how to deal with uncertainty better." He raised his gaze. "I didn't want to get hurt by the possibility of you leaving, so I pushed you away instead."

"I know." She rubbed her thumb in a circle against his palm. "I forgive you, and I hope you'll forgive me for letting my fears get in the way. I was terrified of a making another mistake, so I kept delaying my decision."

"Yes, I forgive you." He leaned across the table and kissed her lips. Not only was she staying, but she was writing. "I can't believe the *Gazette* will publish your essay and pay you." She had let him read the story before they left for dinner. When he stumbled across the final lines about her decision to stay and her love and respect for him, he had pushed aside the laptop and pulled her into his lap for a long, lingering kiss.

"I'm more surprised by the potential job offer," she said, tilting her head. "Part-time work would be perfect with the amount of business the inn will be getting."

"You still want to help?" Roman chuckled. Before they left for dinner, he had checked in three couples.

"Of course," she said, smiling. "You'll need all the help you can get, especially after the article runs." She winked.

A relaxed moment of silence settled between them as the server stopped by to pick up the tab. Roman had let Lian pay. But he insisted on getting the bill next time.

"I don't need change," Lian said, waving with her free hand. "The service and food were excellent."

The fog had burned off the coast, leaving the night dark and clear with just a sliver of moonlight from the waxing crescent moon.

"Ready to go?" Roman asked, releasing her hand.

Nodding, she stood and draped a sweater over her shoulders.

He cupped her lower back with one hand, guiding her down the staircase to the street. The rush of the chattering crowd receded, leaving a hush of silence.

She shivered in the chilled air.

He wrapped an arm around her shoulders and tucked her close to his side. The waves rustled across the shore. He leaned into the softness of her body, and she pressed back against the hardness of his. The rhythm of their footfalls echoed against the sandy path.

Neither one of them spoke.

By the time they reached the inn, the lull of silence followed them up the staircase to the lobby. Inside, the heat felt almost suffocating.

Lian twirled out of his clasp and slipped off the sweater, folding it into the crook of her arm. "I had a wonderful evening," she said at the foot of the staircase.

"It's not over yet," he answered. Grasping her hand, he led her to the second floor. Stopping outside the door of her room, he tipped her chin with a finger and gazed into her eyes. The pupils were so wide and black, he could not see the irises. "Unless you want to say goodnight."

The painstaking moment of silence sent an ache all through his body.

She fumbled with the antique key in her hand, her gaze never leaving his face. "Would you like to come inside?"

"I thought you'd never ask." A crooked smile played at the corners of his lips.

She unlocked the door and stepped inside. Crooking a finger, she beckoned him.

He slipped into the room and shut the door. His pulse skyrocketed against his skin.

Wrapping her arms around his neck, she tugged him close.

The pleasure of her moist lips against his mouth blurred the thought of anything else.

Chapter Twenty-Seven

Lian woke with the weight of Roman's arm circling her waist. She snuggled back into the firmness of his bare chest, the warmth of his body flowing from her head to her feet. The light leaked around the window. For a long moment, she wondered if she should stay in bed or wriggle out of his arms to tiptoe down the stairs to retrieve the paper from the porch. She wanted to feel the crisp newsprint in her hands and read her byline beneath her essay. But the warmth of his bare skin tempted her. She could stay here all day.

"Mmm…" Roman murmured against her ear before nuzzling his nose against her neck.

A shiver of excitement raced down her back and tingled in her legs. She wiggled against him, closing her eyes. The paper could wait.

Only when the smells of coffee and bacon wafted up through the floorboards did Lian finally leave the comfort of Roman's arms.

"I'll meet you downstairs," he said, leaving to shower and change in the carriage house.

Alone, Lian lingered over her morning rituals—soaking in the tub and dressing by the full-length mirror—before descending the staircase to the dining room.

"Good morning, Lian," Rosa said, bustling into the room. "Do you want to see the menu?"

Lian laughed. "No, I'll take the special," she said. After a week, she knew the menu by heart.

While waiting for her tray to arrive, Lian snuck into the library and unfolded the newspaper left on the baby grand piano. With trembling fingers, she viewed the front-page spread. Photos of the inn—from the view of the pink palace from the street to the interior view of one of the many rooms—centered around the fundraising article and Lian's personal essay.

"How does it look?" Roman asked.

Smiling, Lian handed him the paper. "Fabulous."

He nodded, scanning the text and the photographs. "I wish they included a picture of Nana and Pop."

Lian pointed to the bottom of the news article. "Turn to the back."

Flipping over the newspaper, Roman chuckled. "They did."

In the top right corner, a black and white photograph of Davide and Marisa Valentino was displayed along with the rest of the story, including the web address for the crowdfunding site.

"I miss them," Roman said, his eyes misting.

Lian squeezed his arm. "I miss them, too."

The phone rang.

Jolting, Roman handed her the paper and picked up the landline. "Valentino Inn, Roman speaking." He nodded while the caller talked. "Okay, let's see." He tapped on the tablet at the host station. "Yes, I can book you for three nights on Memorial Day weekend."

Lian smiled, returning the paper to the library.

As soon as Roman hung up, the phone rang again. "Valentino Inn, Roman speaking."

Rosa poked her head out of the dining room. "Ah, there you are. Your breakfast is getting cold."

Pointing to Roman, Lian said, "The phone won't stop ringing."

"Are you saying I need to put your breakfast back in the oven?"

"No, I'll be there." She didn't want Rosa to go through any extra trouble for her. She had enough on her plate, serving four additional couples. Maybe Lian would have to become Rosa's right-hand woman to keep up with the demand.

"Sorry about that," Roman said, hanging up the phone. "I'll switch it to voice mail, and call everyone back after breakfast."

"Are you sure?" Lian arched an eyebrow. "You don't want to keep guests waiting, do you?"

He wrapped an arm around her waist. "The only person I don't want to keep waiting is you."

Laughing, she followed him into the dining room. Through the picture windows, she glimpsed the crystal blue sky and the sultry gray waves. Guests ate at the adjacent tables, murmuring amongst themselves. As she sat in the chair Roman pulled out for her, the scent of the bacon and egg frittata mingled with the smell of freshly poured coffee. Placing the cloth napkin across her lap, she glanced up into Roman's soft, brown eyes. Soaking up the feeling of love and belonging, she reached for his hand. Squeezing four times, she said, "I'm here. I care. I love you. And I'm finally home."

Epilogue

One year later

Roman stood in the courtyard dressed in a black-and-white tuxedo with a pink gerbera daisy pinned to the lapel. Glancing at the two dozen guests sitting in folding chairs in the courtyard, he clasped his hands tightly in front of him. The sun had already set. Twinkling white lights woven along the climbing ivy against the pink stucco walls created a lavender haze in the courtyard. The twilight wedding at the inn had been Roman's idea. He wanted his happily-ever-after to begin where he had met his soon-to-be wife.

Over the past year, he and Lian had grown closer while remodeling the inn. Her eye for detail complemented his desire for authenticity. She negotiated good deals on new wallpaper and mattresses, and he found local tradespeople to refinish the hardwood floors and antique furniture. A boost in reservations kicked off their grand reopening this spring. Lian still worked part-time for the local paper but had started writing a travel memoir in her spare time.

Now, waiting for the wedding ceremony to start, Roman trembled from the nervous drumbeat in his chest.

Lian's niece, Bella, stood to the side cradling a violin. She raised the bow and played the opening notes of "Wedding March."

The French doors opened, and Lian stepped out carrying a bouquet of pink gerbera daisies in her hands. She wore a white slip gown and a crown of white daisies in her long dark hair.

Roman gasped. She was so beautiful. He wished Nana and Pop could see her.

Smiling, Lian stepped across the flagstone path between the rows of seats to the altar. She passed Rosa, Roman's father and his family, Roman's mother, his aunt, a couple of his colleagues from school, her two sisters and their families, her parents, and Charlie from next door. She clutched the daisies closer, her gaze focused on Roman who stood at the altar near the fountain, holding out his hand. When she reached his side, she gave her bouquet to her cousin, Geeta, and clasped Roman's fingers.

The minister cleared her throat and began. "Dearly beloved, we are gathered this evening to celebrate the union of two people."

Lian's fingers warmed against his hand as the words the minister spoke resonated in his chest. He smiled. *It's happening. It's really happening.* That little boy who fell in love with the woman beside him was finally seeing his dream come true.

"Do you, Roman, take Lian as your lawfully wedded wife, to love and to cherish, till death do you part?"

Nodding, he caressed Lian's fingers. "I do."

The minister smiled. "And do you, Lian, take Roman as your lawfully wedded husband, to love and to cherish, till death do you part?"

She widened her smile. "I do."

After the minister announced the exchanging of the rings, Roman plucked a gold band from the velvet pillow Lian's nephew, Brian, held. He slid the ring over her cool knuckle. The metal glinted in the twinkling fairy lights.

Lian took a matching ring from Geeta and wiggled it over his knuckle. The thick gold band gleamed against his tanned skin.

The minister nodded. "By the power vested in me by the State of California, I pronounce you husband and wife. You may now kiss the bride."

Blinking back tears, Roman grasped both of Lian's hands and bent his head to graze her lips.

She removed her hands from his clasp and wrapped them around his neck, tugging him close. Her lips parted his lips, and her tongue slipped into his mouth.

A surge of heat shot through his body. He pressed her against him, feeling the edges between them blur. When he finally pulled away, the crowd cheered, and the music started again.

Acknowledgments

Thanks to Martine Inn for providing the lodgings that inspired this story.

Last Chance 208

About the Author

Angela Lam is the author of several books focusing on the lives of modern women struggling to find their place in this ever-changing world. A recipient of residencies at Hedgebrook and Vermont Studio Center, Lam currently teaches fiction writing at Gotham Writers' Workshop.